New Selected Writings of Michael Thomas

New Selected Writings

of

Michael Thomas

Shoestring Book Publishing
Maine, USA

New Selected Writings
of
Michael Thomas

Hardcover

ISBN: 978-1-943974-07-8

Published by: Shoestring Book Publishing

Layout and design by Shoestring Book Publishing

For information address:
Shoestringpublishing4u@gmail.com
www.shoestringbookpublishing.com

Acknowledgements:

This book is dedicated to my publishers, Allan Reed Emery and Alison Wakefield of Shoestring Book Publishing, who exceed the boundaries of protocol by being my mentors, advisors, friends and ultimately the best publishers I could have ever expected to find.

To trust someone who understands words and their power, is to lay the sword down and accept that which is greater by far. My thanks to both of you, Allan and Alison.

Table of Contents

Acknowledgements: v
Chapter One 2
The Rabbi Gets Into A Tangle Over Suicide 2
Chapter Two 9
Rabbi Schlotz's Minute Mystery 9
Chapter Three 13
Rabbi Talks Of Pellerin 13
Chapter Four 15
Rabbi's Poetic Interlude To Joeseph Haydn Symphony 85 in B Flat H 1/85 "La Reine" Romance Allegretto 7:03 Minutes 15
Chapter Five 16
Rabbi Reflects on Religion 16
Chapter Six 18
Rabbi Schlotz and Alter-Ego Rabbi 18
Chapter Seven 22
Rabbi And Michael Dennis Patrick Haag 22
Chapter Eight 25
Rabbi's Ghosts 25
Chapter Nine 27
Rabbi Writes Poetry: Exegesis 27
Chapter Ten 28
Rabbi Listens to Emmylou Harris – 28
Defying Gravity 28
Chapter Eleven 29
Rabbi Explores The I-Ching 29

Hexagram 18-Ku-Work on 29
What Has Been Spoiled [Decay] 29
Chapter Twelve 31
Fighting With The Devil 31
Chapter Thirteen 32
A Rabbi Schlotz Minute Romance 32
Chapter Fourteen 34
Rabbi Remembers Gerhard Woltemade 34
Chapter Fifteen 38
The Rabbi Slips Off The Rails 38
Chapter Sixteen 41
Rabbi Attempts A Character Analysis: 41
Chapter Seventeen 43
Sharon: From The Stories of Rabbi Schlotz 43
Chapter Eighteen 49
Falling 49
Chapter Nineteen 51
Rabbi Attempts to Understand Ervin 51
Chapter Twenty 57
Rabbi's Name 57
Chapter Twenty One 59
Another Rabbi Schlotz Minute Mystery 59
Chapter Twenty Two 60
Rabbi Reflects upon the Michaels Family 60
Chapter 23 62
Rabbi Talks of She Who Has No Name 62
Chapter 24 63
Rabbi Remembers Rocco 63
Extended To All Of Men 63

Chapter 25 65
Rabbi speaks of Tony Nihra and Mike, 65
Rabbi's father 65
Chapter Twenty Six 69
Rabbi Sadness 69
Chapter Twenty Seven 71
Rabbi Talks Of Maria And Larry 71
Chapter Twenty Eight 75
Rabbi discusses Steven Trowbridge 75
Chapter Twenty Nine 77
Rabbi Cries 77
Chapter Thirty 78
Rabbi 'Lets Go' Briefly 78
Chapter Thirty One 81
War 81
Chapter Thirty Two 83
Tony, Sharon and Aunt Irene 83
Chapter Thirty Three 90
Rabbi Pitches A Bitch 90
Chapter Thirty Four 91
Rabbi Talks About His Daughter 91
Chapter Thirty Five 93
Rabbi Gets Silly Poetic 93
Chapter Thirty Six 95
Everything New – A poem by Rabbi 95
Chapter Thirty Seven 96
Anna And Anthony 96
On Viewless Wings 100
(Great Horned Owl, Bubo virginianus) 100

I Try Hard At Patience Toward Ignorance. 103
Lone Poem 104
Forsaken 105
Life 106
Being Reborn 107
New Year's Poem 108
I Wonder 109
A Chant Poem 110
Ancient Lore 111
Heaven 112
I Wanna Be With You 113
The Cat Without A Christmas 114
To Be A Sunday Worshiper 115
Light That Has Survived 116
History 117
My Success Becomes My Failure 118
You Three Times Love 119
We Were 120
The Peacemakers 121
Beatitude Of Mercy 122
River Eyes 123
Precious Memories 124
Forsaken 126
File Me Away 127
Waiting 128
Even as I write at the best, 130
I am the worst. 130
Fire Of My Soul 131
Somewhere; Between A Star 132

And Air I Breathe 132

Religions 133

Two Minute Warning - Fourth And Goal 134

Blood Test 135

Displacement 136

The Rabbi Prays 138

Our Gentle Hearts Throb With Praying 140

Awakening to Hope 141

It's Only A Miracle 142

Being So Mean 143

Vastness 144

Your Smile A Salvation 146

Starting All Over 147

War 148

Through A Silent Moment 150

He Whispered To Me 150

The Forests of Yesterday 151

Everything New 152

What Was Here 153

Jesus And The Blues 154

Red Inside Our Tenuous Lives 156

Footprints 157

Unending Measure 158

Papa and The Moon 160

Alone But Never Lonely 161

Find You Forever 162

Our Burnt Edges 164

A Requiem for the Non-Dead: Prologue 165

A Requiem for the Non-Dead; Part 1 166

A Requiem for the Non-Dead; Part 2 167
A Requiem for the Non-Dead; Part 3 168
Praying To The Gods, or 169
Keeping My Bases Covered 169
Rhyming has Gone Astray 170
We Come Apart 171
Ancient Memories 172
By Death Shall I Conquer – 173
Per Mortem Vicero 173
For Our Children 174
Clarity Of Prayer 176
Oceans 178
Shakespeare Sonnet #1 180
Michael Thomas Sonnet #1 181
Shakespeare Sonnet #2 182
Michael Thomas Sonnet #2 183
Shakespeare Sonnet #3 184
Michael Thomas Sonnet #3 185
Shakespeare Sonnet #4 186
Michael Thomas Sonnet #4 187
Shakespeare Sonnet #5 188
Michael Thomas Sonnet #5 189
Shakespeare Sonnet #6 190
Michael Thomas Sonnet #6 191
Shakespeare Sonnet #7 192
Michael Thomas Sonnet #7 193
Shakespeare Sonnet #8 194
Michael Thomas Sonnet #8 195
Shakespeare Sonnet #9 196

Michael Thomas Sonnet #9 197

Shakespeare Sonnet #10 198

Michael Thomas Sonnet #10 199

Shakespeare Sonnet #11 200

Michael Thomas Sonnet #11 201

Shakespeare Sonnet #12 202

Michael Thomas Sonnet #12 203

Shakespeare Sonnet #13 204

Michael Thomas Sonnet #13 205

Shakespeare Sonnet #14 206

Michael Thomas Sonnet #14 207

Shakespeare Sonnet #15 208

Michael Thomas Sonnet #15 209

Shakespeare Sonnet #16 210

Michael Thomas Sonnet #16 211

Shakespeare Sonnet #17 212

Michael Thomas Sonnet #17 213

Shakespeare Sonnet #18 214

Michael Thomas Sonnet #18 215

Shakespeare Sonnet #116 216

Michael Thomas Sonnet #116 217

Michael Thomas Sonnet #116-B 218

Dante Divine Comedy Mirrored (incomplete) 219

As Michael's Divine Comedy 219

Interlude of Simplicity 243

Poems Of The Rabbi – 256

Patricia, Lewis And Me 256

Chapter One 257

Life 258

Art 259
Music 261
Preludes Op. 28 261
In Fondling Youth Allays 262
Time To Spare 262
Fifty 263
Embarrassment 264
Heat 265
Civil War 267
Only a Memory . . . 268
Waiting 269
Help 271
Moon 272
Hurricane 273
Fear 274
Celebrate 275
Seasons 276
Candy 277
Loose 279
Language 280
Soup 281
Entracte 282
Reaching 283
Breathe 285
Notice 286
Innocence 287
Credo 288
Animus 289
Jaded 291

Crane 292
Psalm of Moon 293
Psalm of Yearning 294
Psalm for Mrs. Haag 295
Psalm for Anna (leaf/ leaves) 296
Psalm of Friendship 297
Psalm for a Bird 298
Psalm of Patricia 299
Psalm of Passing 300
Psalm of Mary Haag 301
Jigging the Twist 302
Extended Thoughts 303
Healing 305
Canticle of Comedy 307
Dying 309
Bring Me Hope 311
New 313
Silence 314
Coincidence of Cloistered Kisses 315
Abounding 316
Away 317
Owl 319
Raptor Accipitiridae 321
The General's Genitals 322
Clutch 323
Joy 326
Indigenous 327
Prayer of Mission 328
Prayer of Cleansing 329

Your Face Has Wisdom To It. 330
Scriabin, Einstein, and Mrs. Tolstoy 331
Potential Date: 333
Dear Sally: 336
Dear Philomena: 339
Dear Philomena 2: 341
To My Fantasy, Florence: 342
Ms. Cornelia 347
Poem For January Thirteen 348
At Four In The Morning 348
He/She 349
A New Year's Poem 352
A Short Snippet Of My Father, 353
Mike Ferris 353
Self-Perception 354
She Who Died Little Known 355
A Poem of Redemption 356
The Blood Widows 358
And Brahma: Brahmavihara 358
Author's Biography: 362
Also by Michael Thomas 363
Please Review! 373

Section 1

New Rabbi Schlotz

Stories

Chapter One

The Rabbi Gets Into A Tangle Over Suicide

The Rabbi wants to commit suicide, such a mess, ambulance drivers to call, relatives and the cleaning up – such a dauntless task. Too bad there is no bottled soda with fizz bubbles to drink for the body to slowly disappear or evaporate into a non-toxic or non-oily smear. He examines the properties of mobility or internal workings all systematically coherent and conjunctive within and without the body. All religions bow before the magic of the execratory function. How terrible to cut short the digestive process by suicide. Rabbi conjures a maxim: "Please commit suicide after taking a good bowel movement" or "Off-Yourself-Herb-Tea"

The invisible creator, be it a messiah, mullah, priest or vaporous intoxicant that swirls around the halo-heavens would balk at suicide destroying the artistry of a life being cut short.

Rabbi is sad and would not actually commit suicide because he feels sorry for his clients who would have to accept inferior CPA service. He thinks about all the hard-nose accountant friends he has who are as impartial as a coconut. He does not want to leave those that depend upon him. At least, not abruptly.

He thinks: Whether or not there is a heaven or hell, there is a tomorrow. There is one more "Pay Day" candy bar to eat with joy. One more of Charlie's pizzas to order and eat with a full stomach. Charlie just got married and Rabbi went to the wedding to speak in favor of pizza and marriage. He officiated the ceremony with a thin crust pepperoni on his mind during the vows. Charlie is an Arab and Hayley, his wife, is a Jew. They were so pleased that all guests left their AK 47's in the vestibule. The most enchanting Dahlia, Hayley's mother, transposed herself in the inimitable comportment of a distracted faire who kept throwing her arms up into the air and cocking her head sideways with her face screwed-to-surprise. She was charming and Rabbi fell in love with her at a distance. Most of both sides of the wedding party thought she was insane. But insanity was subdued by her gaiety. Her laughter swept people into her mood of joy. She was infectiously ceremonious in a dither of abstraction. Rabbi confided to Charlie, "I love your mother-in-law." Charlie said, "Take her please."

Rabbi secretly confessed to himself that these variances in life where worth the show and suicide was out of the question. Rabbi quietly spread his confidence to all the guests by smiling and raising his hand gently with one finger pointed innocently, upward. Unknowing, he was mimicking a picture of Jesus that had been hanging on the wall of the non-demonational church that resembled a Grecian spa with columns and watery angelic oceanic figures painted everywhere. Jesus was held in a trance and indicating where heaven might be in the sky.

Charlie ran the pizza business. His whole family ate off of it. Charlie's dad not only ate pizza every day but he also lived with Charlie for the last few years after his divorce and in the state of mind of being a burden to all those who weakly smiled at him, hoping he would keep out of their way. The old man had aged ungracefully as well as getting married to the assistant cook that gave Charlie time off with her job, filling in for him. She was thirty years younger than the old man and made him look pathetic in public. One is reminded of the 3,000 year old papyrus depicting sexual acts of young women with old men in various positions of nudity.

But, I stray or to stay on point - Sex is a great aphrodisiac as well as a defense against suicide. When one imagines the naked curves of a young women, breast-pointed and ass-rounded, then one's mind is full to the point of not accepting despair. Easy, huh? "It is elementary, my dear Watson." Or as Charlie Chan would say to his son: "A man needs a woman to become a man." Lovely words of the Chinese detective who Rabbi surrendered to reading and enjoying constantly.

Jesus's mother said to her only son: "Being god, you should be able to let someone else be crucified." תויהל
סיהולא, התא רומא תויהל לגוסמ תתל והשימל רחא בלציהל.

Of course, Jesus had to hightail it out of Bethlehem because the wine merchants were demanding payment for the loss of revenue by Jesus changing water into wine. Jesus went to India. He thought to himself, "Why would I allow myself to be hung from a cross ?"

Jesus learned to wait in lines patiently, as part of studying Eastern belief systems. He remembered the story of the maha-thera teacher who told his students: "I bet you all can't wait to piss on my grave." A young samanera monk pipped in: "Sir when that time comes none of us will wait in lines.

Rabbi remembered when his sister was born since he was forced to move in his brother's room. He would go back to look in the crib in wonderment over her tiny size and to renew his hatred for her disrupting his life.

His old bedroom had a view that included bird habitat and the tip end of the alley where he would wait to hear the sound of the basketball being dribbled over the cement and the din of his friends playing and waiting for him to join in. So, this was life, when things were taken away from you without your choice. It was his first lesson in hating his brother and two sisters. He hated their commonness. They not only did not read, they acted as if history and knowledge was nonexistent. This was a time in the Rabbi's life when he realized the lovely words to a song that went: "... people don't live or die, people just float."

See the Rabbi reading night and day. He hates to go to school since it pulls him away from his books. It is as if possibilities were unbounded by literature, painting all types of knowledge that was available through books. The Rabbi had the "Congressional Record" mailed. It was thousands of pages telling what went on in the houses of congress and government meetings every single minute of every day.

It is amazing what can be crammed into our small brains. It is as if the head has no limit to storing all in an place for memory to recall.

Now, what is it that makes thoughts of suicide even come into our heads. The attempt to self-negate one's self is funny. We spend so much energy getting into this world, squeezing through a little hole between a woman's legs. Our first inclination is to cry either out of happiness that we made it out or fear that we have a whole lifetime to get over being born. In an earth over seven billion years old, we celebrate our birthday while the north and south pole laugh at us. What would it be like if each continent as well as the ocean celebrated their birthday each year. The deserts would get drunk on salt water and the moon would wink at the sun in amusement. Africa would light a candle to the Antarctica. The wind would hold its breath against the silence of spaces between the stars.

The Rabbi feels self-indulgent and thinks about hanging himself. He takes a rope into the Manistee National Forest and ignores the birds cautioning him. He pays no attention to the quiet tree canopy that shadows the empty cathedral of his delight. He is on a mission to say goodbye to fern and bracken of forested tree lanes. He is going away, but does not know where. He hopes no one will get in his way. If walkers pass him, he will not look into their eyes because he does not want any conversation leading to his hanging himself. Besides, they would only try to talk him out of it and he is not even sure if he wants to go through with it anyways. You have to understand, even suicides have pride.

The Rabbi is rich, comfortable with himself and yet he is walking with a stupid rope around his shoulders and looking for a sturdy enough tree branch. The Rabbi knows he is going to walk all the way back to his apartment and make dinner. There is not a branch strong enough to carry his weight. Besides, he does not have a horse to kick away from him so that he can get some pull on the noose around his neck. He does not even know how to make a noose.

I think most attempted suicides go unreported because the pity-poor-me souls that attempt it do not have the skills for suicide. The inept ones drink poison or gas themselves in cars with a hose connected to the exhaust. Sylvia Plath probably wanted to pull her head out of the oven at the last minute. Hemmingway's finger accidently jerked and his head went everywhere. His shotgun fall on his left foot giving him a sore toe, which he never felt anyways.

Socrates drank the hemlock even when he could have escaped by ship to save himself. I think Socrates knew that Plato, his pupil, would tell his story, since he never knew how to write, anyways, he only knew how to lecture. His wife chided him to go out and make some money for his family to eat. Socrates had reached the limits of his purpose on the earth for his particular lifetime.

If one believes in the eternal soul that is inviolate and permanent, then one can only believe in a purpose for being on the earth with all of its pain and joys. That purpose is to inhabit a human body chosen over all other forms of cellular structures.

The human body with its mind-body structure is the most accessible for a soul to use when it agrees to the earthly incarnational cycle. Therefore suicide is a free will choice with ramifications that are: to finish the cycle and accept a normal death to finish each cycle out in each body.

The Rabbi concludes that suicide is an escape from completing the normal cycle of a life. The Rabbi concludes that if you commit suicide, then you have to make up the whole life and reach the point where suicide became a choice and you have to decide all-over to not commit suicide. To the Rabbi, it was a tremendous amount of effort to come back on the earth to overcome suicide. Getting past suicide and dying normally is the duty of each soul on the earth. Those that chose suicide have to do it over again. Those that chose suicide are not accepting the fact of their everlasting soul that never dies.

The Rabbi goes back home with his useless rope and keeps hope that the pain of a normal death is less than the pain of coming back onto the world and being born through the small opening that closes the door on eternity for a short lifetime of learning and growing.

Chapter Two

Rabbi Schlotz's Minute Mystery

Detroit Homicide detective Adam Asher was greeted by Rabbi Schlotz and seated. Amos went for cold beers. The inquisitive cat, Master Percy, came out from behind the divan and tested the smells on Asher's shoes – dirty from the rained puddled street side-walk.

Rabbi, "Shalom Aleichem" and he bowed to his old friend.
Asher, "My friend, it is good to see you. I have a file I would like you to look over"

The Rabbi knew it was important since Asher's visits at night were rare. The smell of fresh air cleaned by the summer storm gave off an odor of musk from the cooling ground outside the screened-in patio porch. There was a latent dim flash of the receding lightning display as well as a faint thunder resonant. One could be put at ease by the veil of cricket chirping and the silent night relaxing from the raucous departing storm. These type of storms always reminded Schlotz of Beethoven's Pastoral, number six. He took two beers from Amos and handed one to Asher. Amos took the precaution to wrap the bottles with a cotton cloth to absorb the summer moisture collecting around the bottles. They, all three, toasted each other reverently and drank.

"Tell me about the case." He set the file down and let his hands fall with ease onto his lap.

"I do not think I have ever had such a sad case, my friend. It was a law student, mother of three, found shot in her vehicle. There was blood everywhere. She never revealed the father and the children have not been claimed by any relatives. They are temporarily in the Jewish Children's Home.

In the 1930's Asher's father and Rabbi Schlotz's father were judges and friends. Their social circle chipped in and built two facilities: Brighton Hospital For Alcoholics and the Jewish home for wayward children. Many of the judges friends were heavy drinkers and the hospital was continually a haven for these people. The value of these two facilities was measured by the full occupancy of both facilities and sustained by the generous support of the community.

"Where was the victim's vehicle found?"
"Funny thing. On a side street away from the University. You know, she was going to graduate this year and she had passed the bar exam before-hand."
"Her masters?"
"Yea. Do you want to look over the file?"
"No need to. Give me a couple days and I will get back with you. Let me know if anyone claims the children. Is Ms. White still in charge of the home?"
"Don't make me laugh. Of course she is. She will be there till she dies."

When the two men chuckled at the mention of Ms. White, their memory of their college days together contained the day they both were found playing the piano in the empty auditorium of the children's home. They were playing some Gershwin from Porgy and Bess and Ms. White entered the auditorium. She was a strict authoritarian woman and as she entered the large auditorium, Asher switched to playing hava nagila and Rabbi caught on and followed with his flute to Asher's quick thinking. Ms. White asked what they were playing and they hid the sheet music while confessing to the Jewish folk song. She had a dubious look on her face until Asher asked her to join in and sing with them. She refused and chided them to close the piano key lid when they left. After she left they switched to a bawdy rendition of "I can cook too" from "On The Town" a musical by Leonard Bernstein who also wrote the song. They heard the door of the auditorium open again and they swiftly switched back to hava negila. Ms. White frowned and casting them another doubtful look, she left.

In the morning, Rabbi had Amos pump up the tires on the golf cart and they drove it to the U of D law school on Jefferson Avenue which as an annex of the main school but was the original building of the school before it outgrew the space and moved all except the law school from the building. It was a long day and when Rabbi finished and joined Amos in the golf cart, he handed Rabbi a paper. The Rabbi laughed and they went home.

"Adam. Good morning." Rabbi's voice was thin yet strong over the phone.

"Your murder's name is Gil Davis and he has a tattoo on his right shoulder of a small knife. He can be found at 3018 Seminole in the basement apartment. Be careful, he is armed. Call me when you have him in custody."

Later that evening Asher was again sitting with Rabbi and Amos.

"How the hell did you figure out who the killer was?"

"Did he confess?"

"No, but we found samples of Ms. Twane Smith's hair on the defendant's clothes and we found a gun to match the bullet shell casing found near the door of the victim's car. Rabbi, how did you know the killer?"

Ms. Smith's laptop was at school in her wall locker. Her thesis and her term paper was on the laptop. She was writing on drug dealing. The names and places of her research were all there. She just and got caught up with a deal that went bad and was shot."

"Amazing work, my friend, the chief will be pleased."

"Oh, by the way. Will you please take care of these two tickets?" He handed the tickets to Asher.

Asher: "What the hell! Indecent exposure? Who the hell gets a ticket for indecent exposure? And, to top-it-off, a ticket for illegal parking of a golf cart? What the hell!"

Rabbi: "Amos was waiting long for me yesterday and he went behind a building to urinate. He was caught and the cop gave him a ticket for illegal parking and illegal pissing. Can you get rid of them, please?"

"I will try my best, my friend"

Chapter Three

Rabbi Talks Of Pellerin

Pellerin was in charge of "Billeting" for Fort Greely in Alaska. His wife was beautiful. She answered the door in a white see-through furzy blouse. I delivered the package looking away embarrassed. I often imagined her in that blouse in jail after they arrested her and Pellerin stepping off the airplane in Ft. Sill.

McCarthy never called Pellerin a crook. I used to hate the way the big sergeant snickered at McCarthy and everyone. His desk was next to mine. McCarthy wore the same stripes as Pellerin - three over. The sleeves of Pellerin always had the starch creased exactly down the middle of the bars.

McCarthy ran the warehouse, Pellerin ran Billeting. Often when new personnel were housed, they would stand in front of my desk as the big sergeant interviewed them for the right unit and furniture. Mostly the BOQ or Bachelors Officers Quarters filled the spaces, since not many married soldiers brought their families to Alaska. The families were sectioned off into a set of larger units, close to the size of houses.

When the requisition order got to McCarthy, he always would bring the list to Pellerin and sit while the big man sniffled. I think that Pellerin wished to pick his nose. He sniffled constantly. It was damned aggravating. On top of it all, the big man had a gross mole on his left cheek that took on prominence with his sneer. "Why are you giving Captain Tokuda two couches?" Pellerin, "Mac. Just deliver what I put on the paper, okay?" "Well, you know that people will complain." "Fuck Them. Let them bitch." "They won't bitch to you. They think I decide who gets what." "Mac, I am not going to sit her all day and argue with you. Give Tokuda two couches and leave me alone."

It went like that with every newcomer to the base. McCarthy would see me alone but he never said much about his bickering with Pellerin. He went about his job quietly.

Pellerin always gave parties in his quarters. He would only invite officers, which was suspect in every one's eyes. The rumor was that Pellerin let his wife sleep with the officers as a way of getting his next stripe. I used to think that his wife was a victim. I would always treat her diffidently as a nineteen year old should to a mature woman that pretty. What the hell did I know other than unfulfilled desire.

On the week after Pellerin and his wife left to report to Fort Sill, the news hit. The two of them were arrested by CID or Criminal Investigation Division on a tip from McCarthy. In a warehouse on Fort Sill, Pellerin had secretly stored furniture and appliances that were all under his name for disposition when he rotated back to the states. All of it stolen from the Army. It was my first proximity to real thievery. The cases I came in contact with as a CPA later in life, never had the charisma of Pellerin's case. For years I lay in bed slowly removing the lace blouse from Emily Pellerin's white shoulders. Standing over her oceanic nakedness, I would enter the dream that all men have when their mid-section takes over and suspends them in layman's sexual dervish. When I finished, I would call the guard and have the lady taken back to her cell.

Chapter Four

Rabbi's Poetic Interlude To Joeseph Haydn Symphony 85 in B Flat H 1/85 "La Reine" Romance Allegretto 7:03 Minutes

Dance like the moon hanging itself out to dry in a soft night breeze behind a screen of stars.
Dance, dance like a faire of fantasy in a group of light footed ballerinas turning to the silent wind.
Dance, I am the Rabbi of nothing but lightness and grace in a dither of motion so wistful in airs.
Dance to the incessant pulse of a lilting melody that suspends itself in halting toe steps.
Dance, I am Haydn the humble of notes and spaces between the arpeggios and cadenzas.
Dance I am riddled with uplifting junctures of notes and refreshing flutes between the weave of violins.
https://www.youtube.com/watch?v=xPDkhaKGYMI
https://www.youtube.com/watch?v=xPDkhaKGYMI

Chapter Five

Rabbi Reflects on Religion

They find religion. Or religion finds them. It became the circle that slowly cinches them to a mental death. Anything in their life that they do not understand or are afraid of, they use religion to cover over those anxieties. Use religion to cover over their deficiencies.

Any god that would wish well to a being of its creation would shun religion if it strangles the person's mind. It strangles the thinking using "faith" as an excuse to not delve deeper into meanings and hidden truths.

Adherents who swoon to religions captivation almost cannot stand people who refuse to accept the same faith. They pray for all their associates to find the word and accept the salvation of Jesus reborn. To tell them that Jesus was in India studying Buddhism during any refuted crucifixion would be abhorrent to their thinking.

The world always has professed Messiahs. Crazy people who allow their fixation of being special or in touch with the words of a god, always are around us preaching and praying like hyenas of hysteria. Any religion that winds itself up in fanatic suspension waiting for a messiah to save them from themselves, is a religion of irrelevancy. The great teachers of truth face reincarnation as the best explanation of an existence where we try our best to do good and make up, in succeeding lifetimes, all the things we do bad. How simple and rewarding is reincarnation.

Little do we know the true meaning of Jesus purported to saying, "unless you are born again, you cannot see the Kingdom of God" What loveliness in interpretation. The Eastern religions make each soul responsible for its own salvation by being born over and over till it learns how to behave properly.

Then and only then can the soul go on to other ways of learning its lessons. Only when it has completed the incarnational cycle.

The Rabbi senses a truth so simple that acceptance becomes incredulous. Unless we become like little children we will never enter heaven. Faith becomes something so simple: just act like little children.

Chapter Six

Rabbi Schlotz and Alter-Ego Rabbi

Born of an imaginative need for assistance, Alter-Ego Rabbi bends down and picks up things that Rabbi Schlotz cannot reach. Like when you are trying to carry all groceries in one load from the golfcart, up the stairs , to the kitchen. "Baa baa black sheep. Have you any wool?"

The Rabbi pushes the four bags of groceries up the stairs one-stair-at-a-time. Amos is asleep and he does not to ask for assistance, right now, anyways. He is saving the need to ask Amos for help on another time.

As each bag of groceries makes it way, slowly, up the eighteen stairs, Rabbi Schlotz pretends that Alter-Ego is helping him. In the short ten minutes, up the stairs, Alter-Ego is queried about the decline of the Mongolian Empire which was born of the joining of the Mongol and Turkic tribes by Genghis Khan and all named Khans from 1206 to 1370. Rabbi Ruse says: "Go figure. Think about how each retired Mongol got their foodstuffs from off the backs of camels and into their lodgings. "Whew!"

Alter-Ego Rabbi reminds the Rabbi to slow down and take things easy. "How the hell do we know anything about life? " Rabbi says without words spoken, to Alter-Ego. Life is a mercurial spot of time in the history of seven billion years of earth. Life is an endeavor to refurbish the larders of caves and palatial mansions. Throw out the decaying lettuce. Place the new ball of lettuce in a Tupperware container, sliced in quarters.

Here are the outdated psychological precepts that are forgotten in place of the new viewpoints: The earth goes around the sun, the sun goes around the pivotal axis within the galactic rotating star groups; Freud is replaced by Carl Jung; Chicago is still run by the mob. What the hell can you do? Life is greater than its individual parts. Rabbi is exhausted and drinks a refreshing glass of juice. What would you do when faced with a panorama of thought choices. Would you think of ancient history or put National Public Radio on and hear what is going on at "All Things Considered", one of Rabbi's favorite radio programs. It is a given that all breathing and effort leads toward distinction. The Rabbi tells Rabbi Ruse, "We are forgotten even before we die. Look at the house we live in - The owner died and the relatives have no knowledge of the deed or ownership. The city will not even tear it down because they forgot the house on the tax rolls and when the assessor drives by, she assumes the house is listed on her rolls.

Alter-Ego: "It is very wise of you to make me up as an imaginative friend since I might outlive you."
Rabbi Schlotz: "Very funny - if you are my imagination then you can live forever if you are aware of yourself."
Alter-Ego: "Oh, do not worry. While you sleep, I take all your thoughts and memorize them."
The sadness of life engulfs the Rabbi and he drinks another glass of juice.
The Rabbi thinks. He asks his alter ego, Alter-Ego, this question: "If life can be so beautiful, at times, how can it be so sad?"
Alter-Ego: "All the great thinkers of all time, wrestle with the meaning of life. The most all of them come up with is that life is a mirror of ourselves. We exist because we think we exist. We exist as thoughts that never end. Those thoughts or we need to believe in a greater power or else we would go crazy and our

particular thoughts would dwindle and – that part of the vein of eternity that we supply with our thoughts would die and make all of eternity less because of it. Think how the absence of your thoughts would require a rerouting of all inter-connected thoughts that make up a unified whole. The whole would suffer from your absence. Whether or not there is a god, there is connectivity on a scale huge enough to include all humanity from beginning to its present state. The whole vibrates with every thought and idea ever made. The whole is made up of particles that mass together into groups of regions, groups of stars, galaxies and universes. We are so needed as a part of the whole that, good or bad, is necessary to keep the whole together. Without a part, the whole is incomplete."

Rabbi: "You are wise beyond my thinking friend."

Alter-Ego: "Wise only because you exist for me to be so."

The Rabbi sits back and considers: If all is connected, he remembers the story told of how the Dalai Lama orders a hot dog at a baseball game. He yells down to the vendor with the aluminum box strapped onto his shoulders, "Make me one with everything."

The Rabbi envisions a path to unification of all religions that arises out of the mayhem of a world gone mad. He thinks that the earth and all its various groups have a distinct life that runs its course. At the end of its present course, which was mapped out by Buckminster Fuller as: Phase one: Use of all the earthly recourses of minerals, trees, coal until depletion as a source of energy for humanity. Phase two: Use of the energy of our sun in so many solar ways, until it's supplanted by the Phase three: Use of all the stars energy within the galaxy. Of course, Buckminster Fuller was projecting humanity thousands and thousands of years into the future. The Rabbi is doing the same thing by hoping for unification of all belief systems into one whole that benefits all of humanity to advance without the impedances of various religions. If we all agreed upon the non-existence of a god, then we could progress with science leading us without moral sanctions. Such an amazing book was "Brave New World" by Aldous Huxley which contains elements of possibilities yet to be explored.

Chapter Seven

Rabbi And Michael Dennis Patrick Haag

In the old neighborhood close to the Belle Isle Bridge, where the decay of time crept into the changing street lined with crammed houses that had been worn thin by craggy edged painting and the residue of deserted memories that no longer could fix themselves into concerned individuals – dead ,memories that had not quite died yet – This is where Rabbi Schlotz and Michael Dennis Patrick Haag came to awareness in their final years of grammar school.

Michael's father was a tall kind German descendent of North Dakota Haag's who ran farms after their memories of the old country restarted themselves in the New World. Michael's father was tall and imposing and always seemed to want to reach out and touch those around him with gentleness. He and his mother Martha had two children: Michael and his sister Ilene. Michael was the oldest and became the Rabbi's constant friend. The Rabbi remembers Michael's father for the way he could speak quietly but with genuine power. One day, in the back yard of Michael's house, behind the weak fence separating their neighbor's yard, a large dog was close to jumping the fence while barking viciously. Rabbi was terrified until Mr. Haag went over to the dog who silenced as Mr. Haag put his hand through the fence and pet him behind the ears. The dog moaned out of affection for the hands of this man rubbing him behind the ears. The Rabbi told Michael how amazed he was of his dad's ability to not be scared of the dog. Michael told Rabbi that his dad had been a veterinary in his days in North Dakota.

Rabbi and Michael Dennis Patrick Haag were inseparable friends who stood above the normal peers of their age group. They both were coming-of-age detectives of Mack Avenue and the surrounding streets. They watched and remained above the gangs and cliques so as to protect themselves. There were two small gangs that they belonged to: The Ravens and another group that included Terry Lammie, Dick Storms and Albino Bonooni. These latter ended up in Jackson Prison shortly after grade school.

Rabbi and Michael would keep out of the gang fights but waited at "Effie's Grille" for the gang members to return from fighting and eat at "Effie's". Rabbi and Michael would drink coke and blow cigarette smoke into the coke with straws just to see the bubbles open up and release the white puffs into the air. Effie was a big, no-nonsense woman who favored Rabbi and Michael. She would say to them: "Hey! Got no gang fight tonight? How come you are not drinking tomato juice tonight?"

Dick Storms, Terry Lammie and Albino would arrive with bruises and sit at the booth with Rabbi and Michael who would listen avidly to the details of the gang fight and who won or loss. Rabbi and Michael considered their interest in beating each other up as too dangerous to even consider joining in one of their melees. When asked why they never went to the fights, they would answer that they were too busy reading their books or too tired to fight for nothing.

One summer, Michael went to North Dakota during school break. Michael came back with stories that spellbound the Rabbi. Stories of encounters with loose girls who took their blouses off and allowed Michael to touch them. Stories of how Michael's relatives drove one handed on dirt roads going sixty miles an hour and kicking up a cloud of dust a mile high. Michael retold the story given to him how one of his uncles had pulled the phlegm out of a dying relatives throat and saved the relative from death. There were lovely stories of exaggeration that consumed the imagination of Rabbi and Michael. They both returned to school that year feeling older and wiser from these stories that they experienced vicariously.

Late nights shared by Rabbi and Michael sitting in Michael's fathers car and smoking Lucky Strikes. Michael would pretend to drive and make up situations with built up details of excitement.

Michael had a cousin, Ralph Shreeve, who owned a Chevrolet convertible. Ralph and Michael would drive and Rabbi sat in the back seat. The radio blasting and the neighborhood passing before them as they smoked and pretended a majestic pose of tough veneer until Ralph made them get out and he want on his way.

Michael and Rabbi would watch the late shows on television when everyone else was asleep. It was a magic time of youthful innocence and remains as the imprinted memory of both boys well into manhood.

Michael went to law school and Rabbi into the Army. They lost touch with each other to this day.

The most distinct part of his friendship was the horror of watching Mrs. Haag die of breast cancer over a period of two years as she lay on the bed placed in the living room for the convenience of the family interacting with her and helping her when she needed assistance.

A friendship stays in the memory permanently no matter how time passes.

Chapter Eight

Rabbi's Ghosts

The Rabbi is surrounded by memories. Within depths unimaginable encircled, cinched as if coverlets of experience translated into names, places, emotions that broke open his heart by storms of intense feelings. Like all of us, to various degrees, the Rabbi is composed of situations of moments of realization that can be recalled and imagined all over again and, most importantly, changed by current perception. There are volumes of conversations or silences within this fabric of chance beginnings or endings; A condensing of plots that get mixed up with the changing parts of Rabbi's soul. At any moment in his life, Rabbi Schlotz felt the ease of having everything in its proper place. All details tended to. All decisions made and put in order. A sense of calm pervading.

We are creatures of habitual behavior. We repeat till our mind relaxes.

The sweetness of solitude comes from the resolution of anxieties.

Rabbi never felt comfortable attaching himself to organizations of commonness. Although the association of other souls joining into a united prayer, was a lovely thing as a force stronger than individual prayer. But the solace of singular prayer was strong enough of a force for the Rabbi - sufficiently. The moments of alertness as a thanks for all benefices, was a constant prayer that he engaged in all his waking hours. He would pursue gratitude repeatedly in silent thought as each part of his efforts fit comfortably, into a whole pattern of finality.

The key to overcoming anxious situations was to let the solution come out of his soul by waiting for the answers. The answers always came eventually. He would repeat these words in quintessential thought: 'Thank you spirits for all you have given me'

Here is where the tie-in to universality happened as an outgrowth of minute-by-minute gracefulness - inside the deep recesses of the Rabbi's processional thoughts.

Chapter Nine

Rabbi Writes Poetry: Exegesis

rock speak
child pretend
rabbit talk

eye to eye with forest
billowing visions
buoyant ars poetica

dizzy angels, dusting, devolving
the words of life downward in caches
symbols as music of thoughts
arranged like jewels to the heart

the poet must be bound to truth
sectioning open the soul to love

it is all love: poetry is
guide to majestic madness

textual scriptures of trust

and when I kiss your face
blush beams complex

it is all love, this psalm
to you
adored

Chapter Ten

Rabbi Listens to Emmylou Harris -

Defying Gravity

I melt into silver sounds of light bubbles
Come with me to the aspens leaning over their weight
Into welcoming earth solid in invitation to its family
Growing out of the rain moist soil of worm and bugs

I am a sister to the memory of a grey singing sky
Letting out its heart in soft airs and breezes
I am the complex mixture of words and emotions

Chapter Eleven

Rabbi Explores The I-Ching

Hexagram 18-Ku-Work on

What Has Been Spoiled [Decay]

Oriental Fresco - oldworldartisans. com
The bowl in which the worms breed
to whence despaired must pay heed
open their hearts to a newer creed
becalm, be stilled, to a God-speed

It is a self guilt that is the cause
to whence despaired must pause
open their hearts to God's laws
wrap themselves in love's gauze

Keeping-still mountain, gentle wind
decay of indifference, a will spinned
away from dizzy, to peace impinged
no heaviness, hurt, hate or chagrin

Further one to cross the great waters
three days mourning, three daughters
grace gentle energy fled three quarters
pay the pandemic portentious porters

Six at the beginning setting-right means
a spoiled father, a son departed between
danger, good fortune in the end a queen
will spare the shadows with a sun-screen

There will be little remorse, no one to blame
Slight cause for regret, none for the shame
The hurt will linger, humiliation plays lame
pointed fingers, frowns, sad-faces framed

Suicide sets below serving princes and kings
stepping forward seizing confidence in things
heart will grow magnaminous, soul will sing
now the remains are what the loving brings

Chapter Twelve

Fighting With The Devil

Devil: I will make your mind a muddle. That fine-tuned thinking that you so pride yourself in, I will turn into itself into a swirl of nonsense that has no ledge to firm itself against; No place to cling to in refreshing words or safe ideas. I will bring mayhem to your soul and you will see the obverse side of placidity. You will feel like a tree with no trunk or secure place in the moving earth; A tree with no balance or limbs of grace.

Rabbi: (Giggles)

Chapter Thirteen

A Rabbi Schlotz Minute Romance

She sparkled down the corridors of histories of allurement bound into a woman's curves – a woman's grace innocently sumptuous. Vicki's husband was overseas finishing an enlistment. Rabbi watched every movement she made. He knew that all the men in the office wanted to touch her. She knew also how seductive she was. She kept to herself and shunned Ms. White, the office manager who was openly jealous. Vicki shared reserved laughter with Donna, the receptionist. Mainly, Vicki kept out of the way of the office personnel as a safe bet for avoiding rumor.

Rabbi built up spaces left hanging in the air of her dresses flowing gently as she moved. She was not tall, but pert in her medium build and strong ambiance. She was part Irish German. She had a way of being kind to all. She had the mannerisms of joyfulness so infectious as if her smile kept its radiance long after the moment passed of her amused gaiety.
Years later, Asher asked Rabbi: "Did you fuck Vicki?" The answer was always a lie to keep her safe from scandal.

Yes he fucked Vicki. He fell asleep on her living room floor after dinner. She was so taken by his abandonment of decorum that she woke him naked and put him back to sleep with sex.

The two of them carried on as if they were each taken with laughter as their special attachment. One clerk at the check-out counter said: "You two act as if you have no problems in the whole world. "

The weeks of time passed between their love making and restaurant meals. They took each event as part of a whole of

a sacred communion. They both knew that their time was short before her husband would return. They both knew the time they had was short on both ends of their joy. They left-off and put up no indication of their involvement. They were smart enough to keep up appearances when her husband returned. Days and weeks dissolved and they both smiled as they worked in their secret and they let the memory end in grace and privacy.

Chapter Fourteen

Rabbi Remembers Gerhard Woltemade

Impressionism upon a young Rabbi exerted by his neighbor, Gerhard, was extensive. In the 1970's Gerhard lived in the house he built beside a second identical home that Rabbi lived in. Gerhard would sit with Rabbi year round in the basement or back yard. Gerhard marked his time with Rabbi by pointing to the ground level receding or settling around the bricks of the house. "Each year it goes down. " Rabbi would shake his head and Gerhard would add: "They threw all the junk around the house before they filled it in with dirt. Each year it goes down, believe me. " Rabbi had no reason to not believe Gerhard. Rabbi spoke of the formation of a Grand Canyon, and Gerard would fix a stare at him as if to warn him to not be so funny.

In 1915, Gerhard served under the Wilhelm II in Bremen on the North Sea aboard a training vessel docked permanently. Gerhard was a cook training other cooks for duty at sea for the war effort. Because of his position as the main cook trainee, Gerhard had control over all the food used for training purposes and he shared much of the food with the poor families in town. The trade-off was that the families turned a blind eye to their daughters sleeping with Gerhard in return for larger portions of food. George, (as I called him), would say, at least once a week, with a wink to me, "I had a different girl every night, believe me. " I had no reason to not believe him and I would wink back to him.

The reasons I loved or admired George so much was his skills in all fields. He spent over ten years travelling around Germany, prior to the war, in the apprentice program as a plumber, electrician, carpenter, dry wall installer and builder. He could mostly do anything. Of course, if I started a project, he would investigate and make fun of my fumbling until he would break down and show me the right way to do things. He would always end his instruction with the words, "believe me" for example he would say: "If we started at the end we would have finished sooner, believe me. " And he would laugh uproariously at the time-worn concept, and of course I would always agree and laugh with him.

George raised goldfinches, "Carduelis, Eurasian goldfinches. He and I would travel to buy birds to replenish his cages mainly for birds he would sell. He called them and won awards for the birds he sold out of his various cages in the basement and in the garage. He called them "gouldians" and he would reach the heights of pleasure tending each bird he knew individually by sight. Each time I would sit with him smoking unfiltered, king size, Chesterfield cigarettes, he would get so excited telling me what new indication of behavior one of his birds exhibited, or what bird was in the hospital cage under extra care and how long before they would go back, healthy, to their cage. He had parrots but his joy was the finches. "The finch has every color in the world, believe me. " It never occurred to him that we were both smoking in that small room with all the cages and probably contributed to the death of many of his birds from second hand smoke.

His friend, whom we would visit each week, raised spiders and snakes as well as goldfinches. I remember one visit where his friend took us up to the bathroom and opening the door surprised us with an alligator that he had bought and was raising. George, who could take-or-leave snakes and spiders, expressed concern for his friend being in danger. He told his friend, "You could lose an arm, believe me. " His friend laughed.

There was a bond between George and myself by our talks or quiet visits. When two people share ideas, there is always the borders where charity steps in and one or the other pardons the hidden misconceptions, and goes on with the relationship. Anti-Semitism is such an inset characteristic of peoples formed by ignorance, mainly. George never knew that Rabbi was a Jew. He just knew him as a man and never delved into Rabbi's beliefs. Funny how a relationship can bind itself without details that mean more than the relationship itself. Under friendships or times of stress, there is a breakdown of prejudice and people get comfortable with each other superficially. Or they find another target for their blindness.

George: "If you give a Jew a dollar, they pit fifty cents in the bank to save, believe me. "
Rabbi: "So what? Do you envy their ability to save?"
He would tap his cigarette letting the ash fall on the cold cement floor, and ignore my question.
George: "Someday all those people leaving Detroit for the suburbs will come back, believe me. "
Rabbi: "They ain't never coming back, George. They are gone for good. "
George: "No, they will be back, you see, they overspend with credit cards and they "stretch their feet past the rug, and get cold feet. "

When George died, Rabbi went to the funeral home early before anyone else came to say his goodbyes privately to him with tears. As he lay in the coffin with that wonderful chiseled, tight jawed look so rock-hard and precise with the eyes sewn shut, he placed his hands over George's rough hands and let the spirit of his indomitable nature caricatured by strength, seep into him forever.

Chapter Fifteen

The Rabbi Slips Off The Rails

He is not even a Rabbi. He acts like a theatrical performer who is so good at acting that he even fools himself. The Rabbi has changed religions more often than Hamlet, if Hamlet had been a politician. To pinpoint the Rabbi's code of ethics, look to Friedrich Nietzsche's principal that the most accurate philosophy for anyone is the one that fits their circumstances. Can you believe that? How the hell do you reconcile evil versus good. Does Nietzsche mean that evil is its own self-justification? The Rabbi definitely believes in good over evil. But, the Rabbi tries to understand evil as a temporary back-drop affording those that decide against evil to, ultimately, chose good over evil. In other words, evil is an impetus to the permanent preferred behavior, to act good.

Maybe the rule is that any force needs a counter force in order to define itself. How often did the Rabbi scour at the obese people in line in front of him? He often thinks that eternity would be a hell to be forced to share it with some of the gross people that one comes across in a normal day. The Rabbi pretends to spend a day pushing an empty cart around all the major department stores. He stops people quickly and tells them: "Do you realize how fat and ugly you are?" People become offended and tell him to go to hell. He laughs at them and points to the ceiling saying in fake plain-chant: "Oh Lord of gluttony please look down with favor upon our sister who resembles a whale or a hippopotamus. " Of course, the Rabbi has a weight problem that he struggles with – quid-pro-quo or go-figure.

Rabbi remembers his mother-in-law who was Italian and did not know how to make spaghetti sauce. She was terribly overweight. She always wore a cheap smock. She always flopped along scrapping her flip-flop shoes as she walked. She stunk from her from her flabby skin overlapping and sweating in the creases that could get no air. During a family wedding he was forced to drive her to the reception and he puked out the car window from the smell of her near him. He told his mother-in-law that he had an upset stomach. He considered the benefit of his divorce in double - getting rid of the wife who nagged and her mother who smelled.

The Rabbi decides to put a wrench in society. He creates signs on sticks that say, "FREE" and on garbage day he puts them in the ground in front of the trash bins. All down the street are "FREE" signs. People do not know how to react.

The Rabbi pulls the fire alarm handle and watches the grocery store shoppers rush to get outside. Now, good readers, if you assumed the Rabbi was saintly, well he just slipped off-track for a bit.

Of all things, he calls his ex-wife and leaves a message that god spoke to him in the shower and said that he should get back with her. She does not answer him but he knows what her reaction could be and he does not want to repeat it here.
The Rabbi stalls his car in the middle of a busy intersection and opens the hood and smears a little grease on his nose. People try to offer advice and he tells them that an invisible space ship with invisible space people are examining his engine and taking the information back to their planet.

You would think that the Rabbi would have better things to do but he applies for a job to clean toilets in the Wall Mart and Home Depot. He puts a sign on the toilet doors saying, "Decontamination in process, please wear a mask"

On Sunday, the Rabbi puts on a rubber "Nixon" mask and sits in the front pew acting normal. He pins a paper sign on his back saying, "kick me".
He makes a sign for the back of his car window in oversized letters saying:

"I FEEL SO GOOD SINCE I HAVE GIVEN UP ALL HOPE"

Chapter Sixteen

Rabbi Attempts A Character Analysis:

"She"
Her superfluity bestrides vastness ingenuously
almost like glacial expansion or spacial suns.

One is welcomed by an effusive garishness
like lightness of content that quickly wears.

If pressed to meaning, there would be none
other than an excuse for depth that never
tests the imagination or surpasses emptiness.

Figure what overflows the need for expansion
and write it off as crumbs of comparisons
making a mockery of intellectual reasoning.

One is duped into her world of inventive emptiness.
One becomes quickly disgusted at being ignored.

My mother and her twin were composites of
Similarities that created "argumentative-irrelevance"
like a wind filling the empty spaces between
underdeveloped meanings.Their fulfillment of
promises, never realized, mocked them.

She was, like them, a portent of degree large enough
to hide an underdeveloped assessment of analysis.

Put simply, she is a fool of foppishness.
She is colorless and without measure

She is a librarian, but formless
in never coming up to the high ideals

within the pages of the books she files.

It is as if association with intellectual properties is an excuse for becoming a student of no degree.

It is impossible to like her any more than understanding her.

Chapter Seventeen

Sharon: From The Stories of Rabbi Schlotz

Funny thing about self-image is that the caste system of social standings could be self-imposed in the case of Sharon. She cannot step past the self-deprecation of one who does not want to step past. Her father lives in a bubble of static ennui. He surrounds himself with incomplete projects – actually his whole life is an unfinished project. He is lazy, indifferent to change and the depression of a small house trailer full of boxes of things half-done that fill the whole space he lives in. Sharon, the daughter, follows in his footsteps by wanting the world to supply her needs. She cleans toilets in rest areas. She is comfortable not aspiring to the talents that lay hidden inside her because cleaning toilets is an easy way out of accepting herself. She will not face herself. Her and her father's life are of hiding from themselves. Sharon would have to sacrifice the ease of the moment for the burden of growth that comes in heavy doses of education and learning new higher level tasks over longer periods of time than the short spaced easy job and weekend of self-indulgent nonsense.

The Rabbi sees her as a terrible waste of a life – a life where no great strides are met with effort. Sharon was given the opportunity to step into a professional position for a legal firm entering data without the need, initially, for education. Of course these types of new entry-level jobs only last so long before the system demands that the person grow into higher levels. The system suffers if the person does not grow because the person reaches a level of competence where they become ineffective for the lower task that they perform. Not only does the system suffer, but the person suffers out of boredom with the lower level task. The person is faced with a decision to overcome the boredom and grow into a higher position. That growth is with us always in all the positions that the Rabbi performs or all people perform as they outgrow things and face the internal desire to learn more by hard work and study.

All civilizations crumble from the individual parts of the society not growing. Every group of peoples on the earth, contain the lazy self-destructive persons who account for the demise of their very families and groups. They end up being victims of their own lack of incentives. Rabbi sees no way out of the natural beginnings, developments and end of things. Sharon represents all peoples who want to "float" through the levels of life. They float like logs with no control over their destinies other than the short term struggle for what they can scratch out of the soil of their own destitute gardens.

The Rabbi laughs with Sharon laughing at the world. She truly believes that she has a firm grip on the world when the only grip she has is onto a toilet cleaning brush. Her mother cleans toilets for a living and so does the daughter. The mind-set of toilet cleaners is easy since they do not struggle with larger concepts than piss-n-shit. The smells permeate their souls. The little cracks of dirt filled ceramic corners is where they paint themselves securely. Their skin is yellow beneath the epidermis and their hearts are distracted with water flushing and wash basin bowls dripping faucets. They will lie and destroy that which is given to them as help by denouncing the giver once the gifts end. They have no character since they have no environment to build character upon. They cannot have the pride of attainment other than mopping up other people's wastes. They make the world clean while their insides are dirtier than the muck in their buckets.

The Rabbi is sad for these peoples. He is sad because they have forsaken the promise of their birth. They have truly given up on life and live in some bubble of self-delusion. They are empty shells of what-could-be but-never-is. Their mothers and fathers become the prime example of what they are. They struggle to emulate these empty lives of laziness. If they could do something bad to another person, that makes them feel better about their own inadequacies. They would wish the worst for others because they feel that the world has dealt them the worst. They feel they have no control over the hands that have been dealt them. These peoples wander into the gaming rooms of life with loss written all over their faces. They blame instead of building. They cry instead of joyously laughing. They are dead while walking about pretending to be alive. Their eyes are usually downcast and they hesitate out of hidden fears. They are afraid of themselves and transfer that fear onto all experience that comes their way.

Sharon will announce to the world that she is practicing celibacy while the truth is that she cannot be a lover to anyone. The self-deception of her belief systems doubles back onto her and makes a mockery of a her ability to truly love another person. She could never understand the rule that – in order to love, one must first love themselves. She cannot love herself because the world has given her a disfigured image of herself that she is not pleased with. She thinks she is ugly and therefore the whole world around her is ugly. If she has a slight glimpse of her powers, as a women, they are used incorrectly and without love for others who may be initially attracted to her.

Rabbi watches as she pretends in situations to be weak yet portrays strength when she can get something for nothing. She is truly the false person. The person of double-dealing / double stealing. The person with a black heart and soul who wears thin to all who truly learn what she is like.

When caught in the bind of responsibility of arriving on time to a responsible job, she prefers to arrive late to an irresponsible job. A lazy job where arriving late is accepted just so the government can get someone to keep the toilets clean.

The Rabbi watches all the loving concern for Sharon turned into hatred coming back from her toward the giver. She inflicts anger to cover over the truth of her being ungrateful. In the prophetic scheme of things, "when one despairs the gift, then one become despairing". Sharon's inability to give proper thanks becomes the sword upon which she falls to her death. When one spits into the eye of the giver, then one become blind by their regret and tears.

The Rabbi knows that all things become full circle. The Rabbi saw into the heart of Sharon's father and saw a terrible consequence of despair. The father was damned to his own choices of not growing. And, the Rabbi cried for the sins of the father being visited upon the daughter. The Rabbi looked into the future eyes of the daughter and saw the same despair coming to her from her choices.

Maybe these people cannot make any other choices. But, the Rabbi, believes that all people have the right and responsibility to make better choices for themselves. Why they do not is such a sad mystery to the Rabbi.

The Rabbi is a fool, a total fool for not understanding the base natures of those who inflict their apathy upon others by accusing them falsely. The greatest commandment of all rules of life is to love others as you love yourself. It is the cornerstone of every religion that has ever existed. For Sharon to accuse an innocent person of sexual harassment when that person devoted themselves to teaching her, giving her every possible thing she could need to satisfy all parts of her life, is the total opposite of loving your neighbor as yourself. It is the highest level of despicable behavior. It is so terrible as to warrant the most severe scathing rebuke possible. How this woman, who has been involved in drug dealing and drug use, who has been jailed and left no mark upon the world but her own way of hurting others, how she can face herself and not see the death mask of darkness covering over her childhood innocence with screwed on bleakness, is totally above the Rabbi's perceptions. It is a hollow madness of deep shallow characteristic. She has no redemption but that of pity in her hopelessness.

There is only one thing possible from this senselessness and that is the Rabbi has conducted himself with honor and distinction above the rabble of this child's actions. He has, and this is the central point of the issue, he has done the very best he could ever do, or that any person can do, to love this woman with all the means possible. The very categories or details of checks written or effort given to this woman is the best rebuke possible.

If one considers the maximum of obeying the commandment, one can only come to the conclusion that her actions of depravity contrasted against the Rabbi's actions of generosity are so imbalanced as to exonerate him and denounce her in extreme conclusion.

She is below contempt and he is above honor. Yet how else could the Rabbi act? He is a person of commitment to love aside from any possible sexual inference. The Rabbi is a person who can only be accused of not being depraved toward this woman. He truly acts as if every condition of his actions are a blessing upon her and never a besmirchment. To have never placed her in any corner of imposing his will upon her is his redemption and picture of properness. If universal conditions were to judge he and her, she would be placed in some level of catastrophic censure and he free of blame.

The cloak of madness that conniving people cover themselves with is torn loose and exposes them to such abject denouncement when placed next to the pure love of giving and charity that has been given to them. They never come close to understanding how base and greed consume them below their garrulous emptiness. They are the best examples of the worst of human kindness. They are below consideration of honor. Their kind wilt upon the forests of goodness. They form no strength around the lot of persons of love. They are the reverse of love and cannot even be compared to the compact clay of obdurate ignorance. They are, in their manner, useless slaves of demeaned souls. It is even a waste of time to try to define their natures, because nothing is gained by trying to paint them into a wholesome tableau. The most that can come from interaction with these peoples is to fight to keep from prophetic madness toward them and to still love them as some sediment of possible goodness that might come in a huge expanse of time where they can wash themselves of their lives of possibilities and become what is possible of humanity when they grow past the deserts of their indifference.

Chapter Eighteen

Falling

There is something about balance. Staying on two feet that becomes a measure of ones ambulatory independence. When Hank Woltemade got old, he no longer could stand upright. His embarrassment over calling Tim to pick him up off the floor, gave way to gratitude and Tim would raise him up; Hand him his walking stick and say to him: "Uncle Hank, stay up. " Maggie, Hanks wife, would thank Tim and hand him a couple of bucks. Tim would take it and tell Maggie, "You didn't have to do that", as he pocketed the money.

The Rabbi supposes that examples of various cautious sayings indicating that one has lost their independence could be: "Stay awake", "Watch your step", "Keep your bib on straight. "
No matter how hard he tries, Rabbi drips food on his T-shirt. He likes to wear the ones with patterns so that the stains blend in. He supposes that if he becomes too feeble and unable to do two loads of wash a day, that he could really call himself old.

Stopping for gas, the gas station was rather darkly lit. He filled up and came inside to get the receipt when the pump screen said, "see attendant". The inside of the station had a window that the attendant could have seen the pumps from, if it wasn't for all the cases and sales racks blocking the view. The place was very dark and the attendant seemed to rise up from nowhere behind the counter. For some strange reason, Rabbi imagined the attendant finishing up an episode of masturbation. He was a small young man and his hair was a mess. Rabbi asked him for a receipt for pump "seven" and the kid, in a half kneeling stance, held the edge of the counter and pressed the cash register to print out and hand Rabbi the receipt. Rabbi, deftly, took all six pennies out of the small tray for customers to use when their bill needed extra change. He felt no guilt picking up an additional two pennies from the floor and left to leave. As he stepped out and the door closed behind him, Rabbi fell flat on his elbow and knee onto the dirty asphalt floor. Darkness surrounded him as he struggled to rise up on his two feet. He walked to the car and observed the young clerk walking like a shadow moving toward the rest room – probably to wash his hands from whatever he was doing below the counter of the glassed-in protective screen.

Life was strange. Not a half hour ago, the Rabbi was the center of attention at a party and now, here he is driving home in the dark after having falling with dirty hands, sore knees and sweaty from the exertion. Rabbi imagined that he was one day closer to an "assisted living" situation where there were people around to help him off the floor when he falls. He lets the lights on the street pass him up and his thoughts are pleasing as he thinks of the pennies he will put in the little fat-Buddha bank that was given to him as a gift, but that he never liked and vowed to replace at some time of what is left in his future.

Chapter Nineteen

Rabbi Attempts to Understand Ervin

Truth lies hidden within memory; Half-hidden inside of reflective analysis. The meaning of things comes clearer after time adds to understanding. Time works both ways by eroding experience and clarifying it. The Rabbi fortifies himself with caution while trying to remain charitable and kind towards people.

Ervin once made fun of the Rabbi by ridicule. The Rabbi never forgot the public shame heaped upon him by Ervin. Ervin told readers in his social circle "Get a load of this lover who can guide us with his blowhard advice. He is a true bungler of sorts. " Rabbi never got over the public castigation that marked him to these unknown people.

In time, Ervin's people giggled and forgot the fun that wore off. Ervin was defending a friend who was a sham but too famous to be told the truth. Which, interesting enough is a problem that Ervin has also.

The most important aspect of Ervin's point was being unkind to Rabbi and for that unkindness, the Rabbi never forgot.

TIme passes and Ervin becomes important to the Rabbi and the Rabbi proceeds with caution but with his usual generosity and kindness, except that as Ervin and the Rabbi interact, the Rabbi begins to feel that unkindness seeping back into this situation.

First of all, Ervin never truly says thank you to the Rabbi, unless prompted. The Rabbi knows vocal nuance or tones of voice and how a person sounds is an aspect of their character. Ervin does not have a voice of thankfulness to others or to the Rabbi. No matter how much money or words are spent on Ervin, it never is enough and this relationship never changes for the better.

Ervin is not a person of substance, therefore he has so very little to give back to the Rabbi. It is not that the Rabbi expects commensurate behavior, but only gratitude in small ways, which never comes from Ervin. For over two years, no thank you card, no small gift such as a truly nice pen and pencil set or a box of cigars. Ervin does not even know what might please the Rabbi as a thank you, because he never asks or observes. The Rabbi would be so pleased with a small pack of colored or shaped "Post-It" notes or anything of such measure that indicates thankfulness.

Ervin is a person who reacts rather than acting. The fact that Ervin cannot pay his bills in the normal course of living, is an indication of failing the old test of "going concern" - which is an economic concept that describes a business as either bankrupt or a going concern that can pay its bills in the normal course of business. The term can cross over and be used for an individual.

If we are on the earth and sustaining ourselves then we are obligated, of we are centered or balanced, to pay our bills on our own. Rabbi suspects Ervin of having no place to rent of his own, no cell phone or his own, no steady income and, basically, a mooch. Ervin is so vain as to feel that his super intelligence and sparkling conversation is enough to draw people to him that will pay his way. Ervin is a taker and what he gives back to others is not a well thought out gift to others, but only the bare minimum so as to relieve his guilt by saying he gives people good advice, conversation and his self-adulated presence in return for what they give to him. His relationship with close friends may last as long as the few people who are close to him can live with his shallow nature. He has no car and depends upon others or cabs. He has no computers or equipment other than what the Rabbi bought for him over-and-over. He is basically a bum and the few people who may depend upon him are just enough to make him feel that he is contributing back to society. Ervin is the servant who the master gave money to and he buried it rather than use it to greater advantage. The parable fits him perfectly. Nothing comes from Ervin as a charitable gift. All that comes from him are how he reacts to others problems or dilemmas. And, if he is not asked to react, he will become superfluous as a preacher and go on-and-on as if the person in his presence is totally interested.

The Rabbi asks and asks what Ervin might need and when something becomes obvious, the Rabbi supplies it immediately. Money, things and conversation. Rabbi helps Ervin with business matters and continually steps over the boundaries of what is expected. In the two years, some advertising address labels that were free to Ervin were given for the holiday, to Rabbi. Ervin never forgot to remind Rabbi of the gift, which were part of Ervin's business promotional things that were free from his supplier. Rabbi was reminded of the mailing labels that come free from the AMVETS with an envelope asking for donations. Rabbi gives to Ervin what Rabbi asks about Ervin's needs. Rabbi listens and when Ervin mentions something, Rabbi suggests and gives what Ervin needs to solve his problem. Ervin says that the advice he gives is equal to the things Rabbi gives. Maybe, but Rabbi gives spontaneously out of love and Ervin gives out of the filter of his ego only when asked to give.

Why is it so hard for people to understand generosity? It is so simple that what is given, is given back in some magical way. One never loses by giving, only gains in the process by some magical way.

Ervin does not know that he is selfish. It is beyond his perception of himself. He cannot see who he is therefore he cannot see who or what other people are. While there is little doubt that Ervin is a master psychologist, he fails to understand the simplicity of "Love your neighbor as yourself" His intelligence and wealth of knowledge fail him in the deeper ways of simple kindness.

To increase the interaction with Ervin, Rabbi stands to increase his sorrow over time from this relationship failing for the two of them.

Rabbi, simply decides to keep the business type relationship but be so cautious of the personal one. Rabbi decides to stop being generous because there is no more need to give freely to one who gives back nothing in return. All the money spent on Ervin and equipment supplied to him will be accounted for and put on paper so that the Rabbi does not have to pay tax on his generosity.

Ervin's main line of defense is that he tells people that no matter how deficient their personality is, there is always something good to say about them. He says that all people have the god-spark in them and that is what one should concentrate on when dealing with them. Well, maybe yes or no. One, more importantly, needs to face truth while practicing charity toward others. The best one can say about Ervin is that he is extremely intelligent about the world yet extremely deluded about himself in this world. We hedge out of kindness to try not calling Ervin a fake or false person. We know that Ervin never asked or resolved the simple question asked of children: "What do you want to be when you grow up?" Ervin has never grown up and decided upon a vocation for himself. He is a philosopher who has no philosophy. He is an actor without a contract, stage or reputation. He is a writer who is unrecognized and trying to convince people to recognize him. Rabbi remembers Fritzhof who is a university professor who had tenure at University of Michigan as a philosophy. Fritzhof wrote a book trying to become famous by the book and went around the world trying to convince people that to solve poverty, employers needed to pay their employees for a full year of work and the employees only work half the year for the full year of pay. Fritzhof called the theory: "New Work". He said that employees would use the half year, that they had free, to be creative and add to the world economy a new idea. Go figure! Someone who is a factory worker doing a repetitive task will suddenly become an inventor with time on his hands. Fritzhof gives these people the benefit of the doubt that they won't sit there for half the year; Drink beer and get fat; That they will not waste that half year. Fritzof had his pension and he used his retirement trying to sell his idea to unions and labor organizations. Obviously, he never could and he has become an old man whose teaching days are over and his search for fame eluded him totally. Nor will he be discovered and become renowned after his death. His idea is too impractical to ever be the basis for employer employee relationships.

So, our friend Ervin is the half of Fritzhof's idea - He is a person who spends his whole day, whole year not working but telling everyone that he is a writer and he does not write anything worthwhile but takes from all the world what he needs to live and he is an empty worthless man of no means whatsoever. He is an empty shell of a man and will die without a mark to his name.

The Rabbi is always sad with his inner convictions because, no matter how deep he thinks, there is always the chance that his conclusions are wrong. This chance of being wrong, keeps the Rabbi so insecure of himself while projecting assuredness. Rabbi was born alone and will die alone, so sad but true for all of us, but the Rabbi will die not owing anyone for his life. The Rabbi is an accountant and earns money enough for his efforts. And the Rabbi is a teacher and writer on the side and takes nothing free from the world, but gives what he can. Ervin is fifty six years old and will die having given nothing to the world of himself but an empty soul of chicanery.

Chapter Twenty

Rabbi's Name

Out of the mists of memory where parables and myths are born under the cautions of the poet and the soldier, comes the resonance of soft winds and aromatic scents seeping into all crevices between trees and under leaf and branch.

Here on the frigid escarpments of poles or the burnished luster of desert sands – Here on the fall of treetops cascading across an uneven horizon of distances that escape the imagination, a soft call is heard to the Rabbi being born without a thought upon his soul. The very first thought of the Rabbi is to be loved. Even before he wants to give love to someone, he wants it to fill his little brain from someone or something loving him.

When one enters the world of dreams where each life is independent of the other, each life has no interest in what the other life is doing in its concurrent fashion. The little bubbles of lives float within their births and deaths. The little bubbles are self-contained and it is within the parameters of subjectivity or ego-centered-self that each bubble protects itself from incursion from other bubbles. Only a very high level soul can mix the bubbles up without going insane. That is the reason why people who die, hardly ever return to a dead bubble. Think only of a bee hive that is abandoned because all the cells have given their contents to posterity and their shell is empty and useless.

Dead bubbles are shells where the lessons learned are absorbed within the matrix of the "over-soul" These lessons enhance the "over-soul" and make it either a better "over-soul" or worse depending upon the overall nature of the dead bubble.

Rabbi knows that the "over-soul" is the true person that he and others are. This large bubble of the "over-soul" is the one that the spirt forces are interested in. It is the only person that spirit will inter-act with in terms of evaluating what the soul needs in advice. Spirit will review and analyze the "over-soul" in an objective fashion where each measure of the person is checked against a higher standard of evolution.

Little did Darwin know how pertinent his theory was when applied to the matrix outside the veil of our small bubble of earth.

When the Rabbi wakes from the mists of his "over-soul" he names himself as a teacher because he has no other recollection of being anything but an example for others to follow. He chooses his name outside of the ways of religions and he has a difficult time, when ensconced, within the human body, to find the correct name. Rabbi is a Jack-of-all-trades, soul. He is too proud to call himself "The Pope" because if he did, then he would sell all the art of the Vatican and give the money to eradicate hunger and poverty. Rabbi knows that it would be impossible to eradicate ignorance since stupidity is needed to balance conformity and wisdom. Maybe the art of Rome would be needed when a new soul sees some god and needs to have the example of Michelangelo from which to draw its conception of holiness. Renoir opens his eyes to beauty. Caravaggio bring to the new eyes of the new soul, an explosion of color within real forms of a woman or man or natures inferences.

Chapter Twenty One

Another Rabbi Schlotz Minute Mystery

Adam Asher adjusted his holster beneath his jacket. It always gave him a sense of comfort knowing that he had the weapon as an extension of his ability to deal with danger. He had used his weapon on many times that he kept an inventory of in his memory. The faces of the people he had fired upon kept him awake at times.

Rabbi: Thank you for asking me to help you.
Asher: This case really has me baffled. Do you want me to give you the file for you to look at?
Rabbi: Tell me about it, first.
Asher: The body was found in her garage by her daughter. She was slumped over the steering wheel and the scene was left intact by the police until I got there. Her name is Nancy S. Thomas and she is divorced for over forty years with no contact between her and the ex-husband.
Rabbi: Reason for death?
Asher: My friend, all these years we have known each other and there are always different reasons for people dying. Her death seemed normal until I found a hyperemic needle on the floor beneath the drivers side door. wha

Chapter Twenty Two

Rabbi Reflects upon the Michaels Family

Sadie and Sam had four children, Mike, Joe, Jimmy and Emmaline. Emmaline was the image of her mother with sharp wizened features to her long oval face and deep dark hair that threatened to grow longer than her shoulders and always seemed to look proper hanging over her eyes and shoulders loosely. She was self-secure in an independent manner of intelligence. Of the four children, Emmaline bore the effects of Sadie's fortune with the ease of a woman of distinction. She was beautiful and never wore make-up but had color to her face that seemed to be made up regardless – with a rose colored vivacity that made her stand out as she talked and held her audience in a spell. She was assured and richly comfortable in her clothes, at-ease around people and always upheld her husband in public.

Her brother Mike Michaels died on an unknown street corner and was buried in an unknown grave forever lost to history. Of what Mike looked, he was wan faced, lean and shared the Michael's family adventuresome look. Mike Michael's never married. He left a small hole in the fabric of community where everyone felt regret toward his unfulfilled life. He died of liver failure brought on by cigarettes and alcohol. On occasion, when he showed up at weddings or funerals, he was a charmer and agitated man. He always had a drink in his hands and smoked incessantly. Rabbi remembers how Mike Michael's would eat or drink quickly with his cigarette surrounding him in smoke. When Rabbi asked others as to Mike Michael's home, he was told Mike had no home but lived on the street. The main story of Mike Michaels life was that the Chrysler Corporation would find him, sober him up and pay him to move the big machines in the factory. He had this skill that he took to his sidewalk death.

Joseph Michaels and Jimmy Michaels were the two remaining children of Sadie and Sam. These two brothers were the builders in the family. Joe owned a lumber yard sold houses that he built with his brother, Jimmie. These two men were bald. They were reflective men who thought below and above the common perception of things. They were astute business men. Joe married Thelma and they adopted two children. Jimmie married Jackie, an ex-nun, and they gave the world seven children.

The world runs in strange circles. The last time Rabbi saw Jimmie Michaels was in the back of a church during a funeral service. Rabbi put his hand on Jimmie's shoulder and Jimmie turned to greet Rabbi. Rabbi immediately saw the grief and sorrow labeled onto the face of Jimmie. The story going around was that Jimmie was ostracized from his family from his immoral behavior. Rabbi could only feel such sympathy for this man who could only view his family, sitting in the front pews of the church, from a distance. Jimmie had an empty grieving heart full of regret. Rabbi gave him as much comfort as possible in eye contact and a feeling of empathy. To encapsulate a life surrounded by such sadness, one can only feel sorry for the person. The effects upon a person's life for misdeeds is a solitary problem that cannot be fixed so easily.

Chapter 23

Rabbi Talks of She Who Has No Name

Tell her to go get fucked
she is a busy-body-suck
who will never have luck
because she is so stuck
inside an ego of muck
through which a truck
could never ever pass.

She is a simple-minded fool
full of words stupid, untrue.
She married a man who drew
words from hell's bitter stew;
A characterless ass who knew
nothing of charity or kindness.

She is a cunt of yeast infection.
A witch of bleak benediction.
And if you ask what condition
can favor her insipid diction
tell her no poem or fiction
can come close to her bitch'n.

I will never tell you her name
since her reputation or fame
rests upon her shallow game
of pretending she's no blame
for who she curses or defames.
She is a cock-sucker of shame.

Chapter 24

Rabbi Remembers Rocco

Extended To All Of Men

Men need to feel they are sexually superior and the desire to couple is stronger than the ability to control that desire. Rocco was a veteran of war who survived many bouts of hand-to-hand fighting. He was a man who read well and he had a sense of peace to him that came from all his raw-reality in life.

A predominant feature of Rocco was how he flirted with his sister-in-laws and all women he came into contact with. It was as if the presence of a woman animated him to smile and wink at the ladies. It was an infectious smile that drew you into his joy. One always felt comfortable around Rocco. The image of him dancing at weddings with all the ladies was one of a happy man who could put any woman at ease. Rocco had four children with Dorothy. His children all grew up happy, like their father and their loving mother. The canopy of Rocco and Dorothy's attitudes lay upon the children and kept them free of many guilt's and anxieties.

It was a surprise to Rabbi to hear of Rocco making a forcible pass at one of his nieces. The niece was taken back and told Rocco to please take his hands off of her, as he did, and the incident remained untold till long after Rocco's death. The incident was spoken of by the niece privately to Rabbi and was left alone to remain untold forever. Whether there were other incidents was never spoken of by any of the other nieces in the family. The incident was a small snippet of how desire can overtake a man beyond reason or propriety.

Rabbi placed the bit of knowledge into a minor place in his memory of Rocco. Rocco was a good man and if faced with this one act, I am sure he would have felt guilty, but got over it quickly since nothing came of his actions but a small caution in the mind of the niece. And a caution in the minds of all men who have these tendencies to sex in all its forms.

Rocco died of Alzheimer's and his wife, Dorothy, tried her best to keep him functioning during his lapses. One wonders how the guardian angels deal with souls who arrive through the veil not knowing themselves. Rabbi remembers the words of Jesus, "What is bound on earth is bound in heaven and that which is bound in heaven is bound on earth. "

Chapter 25

Rabbi speaks of Tony Nihra and Mike, Rabbi's father

Tony was an alcoholic. He drank consistently all day long. He was born into a family that survived the depression without a father to provide for him and his seven siblings. Tony and his brothers and sisters held together and sustained their mother as a joint effort of love. The family cleaned toilets for the church and neighbors. They did laundry and ironed to make enough money to buy food and goods. Rabbi's uncle Tony was a hard working man who looked for ways to get rich easy. He managed to open a nightclub in Detroit called the "Club Manhattan" . For seven years he drew attendance with singers and comedians. The bar had a glass swimming pool backdrop and naked women swam smiling at the drinkers. Tony was a short man with very nervous eyes that shifted when face-to-face with a speaker. The family helped Tony and as he operated without paying his federal or state taxes, the family was always left without being paid. The club did well but had a short cycle of business and eventually closed to the disgrace of all the family and Tony. Rabbi was young and he heard the hushed stories and saw the demise of this venture as inflicting all members of the family. Tony avoided the taxes and became indebted to the point where he could not put any assets in his name. He switched to selling used cars in a shabby neighborhood of Detroit on Mack Avenue in a dirty old empty lot with soiled banners flying on bent poles leaning with the wind. Rabbi always felt the decrepit nature of the lot as despondent. "A & N Motor Sales" was plastered on a wood sign attached to an older pole in the front of the lot. Tony would buy his cars from "Raynal Brothers Dodge. The cars Raynal sold to Tony were the ones that did not run. Tony would pay five or ten dollars for these "junkers", as they were called. He would tow them on a rope and try to get them started so that he could sell them for two or three hundred dollars to the indigent people who lived on the broken down streets surrounding the car lot. If he could get one hundred dollars down, that was all that he would ever get for the car and he never got more. The way he made up the difference was to reposes the cars and sell them all over again.

Rabbi remembers every Sunday when Tony would get Rabbi's father to help him tow cars early in the morning with a chain or rope. Many times Rabbi, as an adolescent, would sit in the back seat as the two grown-ups pulled reposed cars. The cars always banged into one another as Tony and Rabbi's father tried to brake in synch. They never did. The Rabbi felt like a side show circus as the two men would hurry and slow down and bang into each other like fools. At one point, Tony would put an old tire tied to the trunk of his car so the towed car would not damage the front car too much. It was a funny situation because the two men acted with seriousness yet never saw the comedy in their actions.

Tony eventually got in tax trouble with "A & N Motor Sales" and the government could not shut him down since there was so little to be gained by a poor car lot in the ghetto being closed.

It was years later when Tony moved from Detroit with his wife Albina. He moved to Florida and became a car sales person for a large company in Florida. As he got older, he became stable and earned honest money selling cars for a salary. He was always funny to Rabbi and on one trip back to Detroit to visit his family, Tony went around with a photo album showing every one, who would pay attention to him, pictures of his closet in Florida with all the shoes and suits that he had earned by selling cars. He was so proud of his wardrobe as a sign of his success. Rabbi would praise Tony and feel so glad for this uncle who had measured his losses in life against a closet of suits and shoes. To Rabbi, Tony was a mystery of off-centered values. Rabbi often prayed for Tony to find peace within his heart of a life of so many troubles.

Joe Michaels married Rabbi's aunt Thelma. Joe, like Tony tried to become successful after the war ended in 1945. Joe Michaels and Thelma could not have children. There was a story of Thelma being raped and not being able to give birth. The marriage was one of disparity. Joe would constantly berate Thelma in public with words like, "Thelma, I cannot believe a person as intelligent as you can not understand... . " Joe did this constantly and Thelma would defend herself while Joe listened but was never convinced of Thelma's understanding. Thelma and Joe lived unsettled on money borrowed from every relative they could borrow from. The two of them started out with a new business venture called "Cadillac Detroit Lumber Company" on Groesbeck Highway. Once again, the family pitched in and tried helping the venture. Rabbi saw Thelma and Joe take trips down south to buy large lots of lumber. The actual lumber yard was impressive and, for a time, it seemed like it would pay off big for Joe and Thelma, but the venture want bankrupt from contractors not paying for their large lumber purchases. The members of the family that helped out never got paid and this company also was looked upon with disgrace by all the family.

Joe and Thelma tried buying and selling land with little success. Their large land purchases seemed to stagnate with no developers interested. Joe and Thelma owe everyone. The partners in their land ownership tried to take over the land parcels without paying Joe and Thelma. Eventually Rabbi's uncle Joe died of kidney failure from two bad kidneys that deteriorated from too much liquor. Thelma hung onto the land barely paying the taxes till, when she passed, her daughter sold the land at a large loss. It was a silent telling between members of the family who came away without ever being paid the loans they made to Joe and Thelma. Rabbi wondered what lay for Joe and Thelma on the other side of the veil. How does a life of debt become a life of peace in death? Once more, Rabbi watched and prayed for himself and the people he saw with so many problems.

It is a short telling that Rabbi never placed any value on money or fame. He always seemed to have money for all the things he needed. He always found ways to give all his money away without hurting his comfort levels. He never had savings or investments. Besides his health insurance, Rabbi had a long term health policy that would pay for him in a nursing home along with social security. For all the years of paying this policy, Rabbi conjectured that he probably would die without ever taking advantage of the insurance. It did not matter. All that mattered to Rabbi was the chances that he took advantage of giving things to people. Rabbi would have visitors admire an artifact or piece of furniture and he would make sure they left his house with what they admired. To Rabbi, he would only give away things that he loved because he wanted the recipient to have something that he liked. Giving and receiving thanks was all that mattered to the Rabbi's conscious.

Chapter Twenty Six

Rabbi Sadness

For all of us there is the lonely space of emptiness that makes up our separate lives. Amidst the clamor and ballyhoo of life, we are so completely by ourselves. Rabbi has seen this: A priest in bed in a nursing home. This priest must have been of some note since the visitors he had were nuns who filled his water and adjusted the classical music playing on his device atop the table near his bed. The priest never woke or acknowledged the visitors. He remained immobile and indifferent to the very things that made up his life. He was alone with death. He was making his reconciliations with the events in his life. He was conducting his own last judgment. It is interesting to wonder whether this priest was taking to an embodied spirit that was conducting him through the journey from life on earth to life across the veil. Rabbi remembers "What is bound on earth is bound in heaven. What is bound in heaven is bound on earth. " If reincarnation is plausible, it implies that we are in control of ourselves and, therefore, in control of who we conjure up on earth and in heaven.

In a book – "Seth Speaks" by Jane Roberts, a stipulation is made that upon death, a soul was faced with a creation of a struggle with a wild beast and that at the end of the struggle, the soul had learned his lesson or removed his fear of the wild beast. In another example, a soul was faced with the visage of his enemy who threatened him with sword poised. At the end of this encounter, the soul learned to understand his enemy and reconciled his hatred by the "after life" encounter.

Rabbi has often wished for things so hard that his wish almost always comes true. If our thoughts are sublimated wishes.

Chapter Twenty Seven

Rabbi Talks Of Melanie And Leroy

The rabbi has slowly built up a life of giving to others. It is a compendium of his soul piece-by-piece. His thoughts always center upon the benefice of earth and nature's extreme beauty and disasters. He cannot help but to be what his constitution deems.

Larry, rabbi's brother-in-law, is the opposite. Leroy's mother's personality constituted characteristics that Leroy held similar. Rabbi's parents never held sway over Rabbi. Rabbi left home at age fourteen and never looked back. Leroy never broke his ties with his mother, even after her death, she had given Leroy / And Leroy had accepted, his way of life. Rabbi remembers when his mother realized that her naked body aroused his feelings, and she immediately severed her child from her by never letting him in her presence while she dressed. Leroy's mother constricted her son by holding him to her both emotionally and physically. Leroy's mother gave birth to a boy out of wedlock. She could not have aborted the child because of her religious beliefs. She put the child up for adoption and never spoke of the child ever again. She married Anthony, a very gentle but extremely weak man. She totally dominated the man and proceeded with her life with that secret haunting her till she died. Leroy was an only son with one sister. Leroy's mother fondled her son with the normal love of a mother with the exception that she sexually attached the child to her. She never pushed him away so that he could learn love from another woman. She kept him secure by touching him physically and mentally. Leroy accepted this closeness because he was of the same nature as his mother. He accepted this closeness because he was too weak to step past his mother's influence. He needed the attachment as well as his mother needing the attachment.

So, Leroy followed the suggestions of living in an exclusive neighborhood; Of going to an exclusive school; And obtaining an exclusive profession of engineer so that her influence led him to work for the most exclusive company – General Motors – as a chemical engineer. She taught him to be a miser and not spend his money. She taught him to buy a house and live in it alone. She cleaned his house and made his meals. The only thing she could not do was move into the house with him, openly, so she remained outside the house as a surrogate wife. The effects of this relationship made Larry totally uncontrollable emotionally if anything went astray in his life. He would react to simple problems by screaming and throwing things as a way of exhibiting his frustration. His mother was always there to solve his anger and calm him. This condition can be classified as a form of quiet autism or asperser's syndrome – a mental disorder that was tolerable within a life of seeming normality.

How often the rabbi saw degenerative aspects of those around him, that never consumed the person, but stopped the person from leading a "clear" life fully. This was Leroy's condition and because he never broke from this accepted way of life, it became the foundation of his existence and would be that way both in his marriage to Melanie and his ultimate death.

Melanie realized this part of Leroy and accepted the role of becoming his mother and wife. She learned to help him cope with his spontaneous anger. She waited for his rage to subside and she softly spoke to him that she could take care of the issues that beset him.

Melanie's situation was the tail end of her following a set of religious beliefs that she imposed upon her daughter's drug addiction to very little effect. Melanie threw herself into a false relationship with a parish priest and the intimacy lent itself to her avoiding a meaningful relationship. She guided the priest in parish affairs which included being instrumental in having the church buy a small house near the rectory and helping the priest make it a home. It was through the church that she met Leroy.

When Leroy realized that he had Melanie to fill the role of his mother, he half-heartedly pretended to break with his mother – superficially. His mother retained her influence except that now, Leroy made his wife understand that he was under her protection and not under the influence of his mother. But, in effect, the mother still controlled him through Melanie.

Melanie proved her love to her husband by becoming a miser and treating her friends the same way that Leroy treated his friends, with unkindness and abject indifference. With this aspect of their marriage in cohesion, Leroy entrusted her with his money. She only used it to please him and herself and never to please others. Their holidays were filled with decorations but totally void of gifts or joy to others. It was as if a page of some magazine became the fixtures of their house and nobody was present in the perfection of a false picture of propriety. It was an empty house with no presents under their many Christmas trees. No love whatsoever filling the empty lonely spaces of loveliness with cheer. It was a typical Charles Dickens bleak picture of sadness, that the author often painted before he introduced the characters and situations that reversed the emptiness with love.

Leroyy and Melanie denied the court's request that they take responsibility for their three grandchildren, who, eventually, became wards for adoption.
Leroy and Melanie went on multiple trips around the world and shared their memories with their false church friends who came-and-went in their shallow life. None of their friends came close to Leroy and Melanie. All of them realized that none of them could ever share the closeness of a true friendship with Leroy and Melanie. This life of community ascendency became a life of soul descent. There was no soul in Leroy and Melanie's heart. They never invested in the piece-by-piece composition of a soul. They denied the soul and loved only themselves; Loved only their money themselves; Loved only their possessions themselves. They became, as Matthew said: Whited Sepulchers – beautiful on the outside but on the inside are full of the bones of the dead and everything unclean.
Rabbi found this analysis of his sister and her husband, so distasteful. He wanted them to be as pure and holy, as he wished them to be. He knew they did not have the time and disposition to change and that they would die incomplete people who would have to make up their life of incompleteness. And that was his love for them: That they would find a path on the other side of the veil and be able to pursue that path as a way of redemptive reincarnation.

Chapter Twenty Eight

Rabbi discusses Steven Trowbridge

As in all Rabbi's thoughts, he wishes for the very best for other people. Cautiously avoiding anger or ill will, Rabbi is burdened with excessive analysis in his attempts to understand the deepest truth about a situation. In the back of all Rabbi's thoughts is the fact that we see ourselves. Others see us. And God sees us. God being some over soul or souls above us in understanding.

Steven Trowbridge is a client of Rabbi. Or rather was a client. Two years ago, Rabbi refused to help him further because the client did not want to pay. Steven needed tax work, estate planning trust work, tax tangles straightened out. The fee for all this complicated work was not too high, but Steven did not want to pay and Rabbi sent him away. Two years go by and Steven contacts Rabbi asking to reestablish his business relationship. Rabbi has meetings with Steven and realizes these things about Steven:

He has huge added problems added to the first list that were never solved. Steven lies to Rabbi and says that he was the one who left two years ago. Steven lies to Rabbi and says that Rabbi, two years ago, was overcharging in order to pay for Rabbi's problems.

The funny part of Rabbi being a CPA is that Rabbi also needs to be a discerning psychologist. Steven is the type of person who must construe or alter reality in his favor to keep his ego intact.

Rabbi, for a second time, tells Steven that he cannot help him and Steven, of course, gets mad and says unkind things to Rabbi. Rabbi never answers but puts Steven in the back of his mind, once more, and resigns himself to let the thought of Steven dissolve with time.

Steven has earned much money, but now, it is in his corporation and the new problem is how to get the money out of the corporation and into his hands. There is always a tax event to this situation. Steven does not want to face the tax event because he understands it will cost him.

What is so sad about Steven is that he lies to himself, is a miser and his problems never get solved because he does not want to face them.

The words – "To thine own self be true" fit Steven. He cannot see himself or face the truth.

We have a world of people who cannot face themselves because it would demand tearing away the ego and redefining self with so much effort.

In a book the Rabbi read years ago, the author stipulated that the one foremost problem with humanity is the ego that keeps the truth buried deep.

To look past the ego, one has to face how stupid we act. To have over five hundred thousand dollars and not want to spend two or three thousand on solving problems that will keep the money safe, is so foolhardy. Rabbi has learned one truth: If we spend money generously, some god gives us back in hundred folds. Life is an effort is trusting that generosity is loving yourself and loving your neighbor in similar fashion.

Chapter Twenty Nine

Rabbi Cries

For all the things done to obtain love, the Rabbi cries. He cries in his loneliness. He cries in his depression. He cries for sins he imagines.

Rabbi never received approval for himself from his mother. When Rabbi reached age ten he broke with is mother and sweltered under her outward ridiculing of him. His mother berated, criticized, denied any approval toward her son. Rabbi was the first born of four and therefore he was the most accessible of all her children.

Chapter Thirty

Rabbi 'Lets Go' Briefly

A client, that I rid myself of two years ago, wants to come back to me. I tell him to set up an appointment with my partner and I will comply. He cannot find his last year's tax return, which I need in order to help him. He keeps changing the time of the appointment till it becomes impossible to keep on our end.

Sometimes it is hard to hold myself in and I want to speak out the truth. This guy is a mess. His email is full of quotes from ancient proverbs and he cannot keep an appointment. Years ago he claims he left me.

When I left him years ago he said, "So you are going to desert me?" I said, in so many words, I can't seem to be able to work with you. How can I work with him? He tries referring his mother to me. She was married to a photographer and I knew the both of them back in the 1960's.

I remember getting high on hashish and sitting on their front porch with them. The dad said to me, "Aren't the wildflowers nice?" I thought to myself. Is this jerk kidding? The yard was all weeds with Burdock and Thistle overgrowing the scraggly crap that tries to compete with the taller crap that is unidentifiable by any Linnaeus nomenclature. This was the fat father of my "would-be" client. The father, who is too lazy to cut his grass, tries to save face by calling it wildflowers? Back in the 1960's I wanted to laugh out loud at him.

The family carries on their tradition of egotistical ignorance (arrogance). I know the father was his step-father, but I also know that - like kind attract each other.

This "would-be" dunce says to me that I was over-billing him to pay for my employees. Where in the holy halls of hell does he even come close to understanding that I was billing him correctly and he just did not want to pay? Reality is so elusive for some. So, I kindly tell him, a second time, that I cannot work with him and the man unloads all kind of false accusations against me. He creates another bunch of lies and excuses, like his father would do, to justify himself without considering that his accusations are exactly the problem. It is a case of self-incrimination without him being aware of it.

It is now a couple days gone and he is, once more, out of my life. I feel bad because I know his problems and I know how to solve them. One of his false accusations is that: I created his problems. Can you vastly imagine what balderdash this man conjures to say that I create his problems? What simplistic thinking, that I sit in my office waving my pencil for two years dreaming of ways to create his problems. He is so deluded that his condition actually borders on paranoia. He needs to be committed by minimal standards of psychological care. I would venture to say that he will reach the level of blindness that his father reached as his father passed the hash pipe to me and smiled at the weeds with glum satisfaction like an ignorant orangutan surveying for fertile females.

I am sure that this guy will try to get the last word in by coming up with something in his favor. That is the way a self-deluded person deals with protecting their delusions and fixing it so they can feel good about themselves. So, whatever he comes up with I just have to know that I can never win with this person. He will never understand the words of Robert Burns, the poet, "Oh would some power give us the power to see ourselves. It would from many a fault free us. . . . "

I also hate writing this kind of thing because there is so much truth of self-revelation when one tries to reveal other people.

Chapter Thirty One

War

At the start it was fun as a young man's fantasy of adventure. Like high school sports recognition for the exceptional - war was the giving back for family members who returned from Europe World War II, with a sense of pride.

The delving into the unknown of volunteering for Vietnam without any concept of Asian peoples culture or history. The French being driven out of South East Asia was a "non-sequitur" to the ignorance of us soldiers.

In the orientation room, upon landing in Vietnam, incoming soldiers were given prophylactics and told to keep from having children. No mention was made of fighting conditions or terrain. It amazed me that sex was more important than fighting.

We flew into the isolated army base by helicopter. Our assignments were handed out and each of us established ourselves in the barracks quarters.

Vietnam is an oasis of Asian loveliness with rich green rubber plantations, distant horizons of rice paddy beauty spread like a water-spill into the low areas of the greenish fresh land. Water buffalo stood up to their bellies submerged. Half naked people bent over pulling rice out of the mirrored shimmering puddled surfaces. Figures with sun shield round straw hats looked up as we walked past. We would learn, later, how these people lived without any of the conveniences we are used to.

Each living hut was occupied by men sorted out by their occupation. All the belly gunners who rode astride the helicopter open doors with their guns on mounts, lived in one barracks. The ground troops, who went out on patrol each day, lived in another barracks. The army called these small barracks "hooches". The army had a name for everything. I remember how social contact was held in meetings in one particular hooch when men got together and oiled and cleaned their guns. The banter and exchange of firearms took place while they drank and smoked. Everybody on the compound seemed to relish having sidearms strapped on their waist as they walked around all day. It was as if they were cowboys and guns were their self-security.

In another particular hooch it was a regular weekly slide show or movie of all the people that had been killed during the week. Men would relish looking at images of dead boys and soldiers tied up and heads hanging down or shot off. It was the most gruesome unholy thing I ever encountered. It was total barbarism.

There are so many stories in my memory of nights of flares, red tracer bullets leaving a trail of lines where bullets found their targets. I spent one whole year with this fighting and nothing in my life compared to finally flying home to try to forget the noise and mayhem and dead bodies.

Chapter Thirty Two

Timmy, Shanon and Aunt Ida

Sanctimonious, supercilious, slippery worms of a patented emptiness; they have had their eyes eaten by harpies, like Prometheus chained to a rock, then their sockets fill in with a radish pale sunrise every morning for eternity.

Arrogance of indifference; pompous ignorance when lack of knowledge is an excuse for feeling superior to others. How it hurts to have those snide remarks and curtness leveled at Rabbi instead of love and kindness.

The Rabbi comes to the realization that Shanon and Timmy have always been critical and negative toward the world. It is not something new. He remembers the falsity when they first paired off with each other. They never gave back to those around them. Their expressions of disgust were the hallmark of their personalities. They created what Kurt Vonnegut called a "Sineclosure" or a complicit pact with each other to defend themselves against any objective analysis. They simply attach themselves so closely as to let no air between themselves.

Here is how the Rabbi hurts: That for all his life he considered Shanon and Timmy his friends. Only to suddenly understand that they are not disposed towards him. He is crestfallen by having to downgrade their place in his life as less than he wished they would be.

Timmy grew up with Rabbi. Timmy did not serve in the military. To Rabbi, serving was thanking his country for all the wonderful things that were given to him.

Timmy and Shanon are not thankful for what they have. They never express gratitude. They complain about everything. Timmy and Shanon never went on to school to better themselves. They remained at a level of intelligence that typified the parable of Jesus where three servants of the master were each given money. The first servant wisely invested it. The second kept it even. While the third servant buried the money and wasted it.

The Rabbi hates to describe people as out-of-control, because the Rabbi indulges himself in food and drink and resembles a fat complacent Buddha. Shanon and Timmy are heavy fat people whose weight is not carried with attraction. They are people whose weight builds up around their face and blots out their beautiful natures. Their weight is oppressive and makes their facial composite ugly.

Timmy and Shanon have never learned the lesson that: "If you can't say something nice, then do not say anything at all. "
The great axiom of Alexander Pope: "A little learning is a dangerous thing: Drink deep, or taste not the Pierian spring." applies to Timmy and Shanon. They are shallow enervated people with very little substance. Paper thin people whose existence costs more than their substance can be valued at.
If they could possibly mount a defense, it would pale compared to their accusers.

It is a fact that their pride over staying married turns outward into derision toward Rabbi, who got divorced. They assume this level of grandiose just because they stayed married. It is as if duration alone can account for their false esteem. Most people who brag that they stayed married for commendable amounts of time, really do not have any growth in their lives. They endure out of complacency.

So, the Rabbi wishes these two people well. They will never share the joy of the Rabbi's attention. They will shrivel and leave nothing but a dissolving blot on the earth that sustained them. The feeling of disgust remains in my heart as an aftermath of being around my family for the party for Aunt Ida. All my life, from the time of being a little boy, I have had that same feeling of disgust from being around my family.

"The feeling stems from my family being rigid Catholics and not having any spiritual values at all." Rabbi said. "My family are unkind. They never make me feel good about myself. And they go out of their way to be cruel. Not one of them truly follows the teachings of Jesus whatsoever."

He has a term for their behavior: "I call them Catholic Monsters."

"Believing in Buddhism is simple: I believe we all come back to the earth to work out our deficiencies.

I do not believe in a heaven or hell. I do not believe in a crucifixion to salvation.

I believe all of us on the earth create our own salvation by reincarnating over and over till be get it right and will be done with the "Earth Recycle Program".

Where we go once that is done, is simple. The god has other ways for us to grow spiritually in other places and other choices.

I believe we are always in control of all of our choices."

"I used to ask Florence, my mother, why do you love me? She would say, Why do I need a reason for loving you, you are my son and that is enough. I said, do you love me because I am a CPA, Writer, Kind Person. She said Alastor, quit being silly. I have to love you because you are my son, that's it. My mother never loved me, she loved herself for me being her son. How sad. She was never proud of me, she was proud of herself for giving birth to me."

"Aunt Ida has never been nice to me. She has never thanked me for helping her and Uncle Jack for all the free work I did on their house at 2753 Chambers. I spent years being Jack's assistant every day for weeks upon weeks as he remodeled that house with my help. I was young and had a car and drove everywhere to get his supplies. I scrounged wood and plasterboard at every construction site possible. I was working for the Big Bear supermarket on Mack Avenue and I brought to Ida and Jack all the damaged canned goods every day. Box and box of lovely canned goods with their labels lost. Irene and I would go through each can to determine what was inside. It was a labor of love, since I loved both of them from the bottom of my heart."

The two of them simply ignored the simple mechanics of thanking him. He went into the army and came home, married and divorced and the two of them never once thanked him, since they spent their time grieving over the loss of Jenson, their son, who died of Aids complications. It was as if they had never once acknowledged that he was the only true son they had. Such short sighted people, as they were.

At some point in his development, Rabbi became a CPA and Ida had him doing her tax returns. She would not pay him and when her work got so complicated, he simply told her he would not do it any more for free.

She left him with anger and he thought to himself: "How cruel of her to expect me to work for nothing, like I did on her house". That has been the extent of his relationship with her and her husband. They never once acknowledged him and they always cast aspersions upon him for his odd behavior as if he was anathema to their Catholic world.

Years later, Rabbi had an article printed in a famous magazine. The article was on accounting. Ida called him and asked if he was the author. She hummed and never, never congratulated him for being published. Now, with nine books at Amazon for sale she and the whole family simply ignore congratulating Rabbi for his successes. He has learned to segregate his feelings from his family into an area of his mind where they reside as inconsequential and a small part of his memory. They are not important to him at all. But, being around them for even a few hours, revives his feelings of sadness over their selfishness.

They are immersed within their madness like wild animals who have no conscious or souls. They are cruel and self-absorbed to the point of being inhuman. They have unsubstantiated souls that are darkened from lack of kindness. A soul is made up of bit-by-bit situations of love extended to others. Their souls are dead and their hearts are graphite, immutable, pitch-black. Their souls reside in the swirl of anger and hatred where hearts languish in obscurity. They are consciousness recently emerged from the realm of infinite possibility. They are new, unfinished souls of immaturity. They are insulated from the wellness of love and charity of Jesus, Buddha, Mohammad and Confucius. They are barbarians of bitterness. They are dis-related from humanity in the most auspicious elements of goodness and heartfelt grace. They are particles of perdition. Their life's are mostly worthless and will all have to done over and over till they get it right. Rabbi can only pray for them in their unworthy way and hope a god will hear my prayers for them to try to help them. But, they are not part of his life in any way. There is no way any of them could ever describe the Rabbi since he hardly knows himself, but he tries so hard to be kind and loving and thankful to the earth for all that is given to me. He is a rich pauper of cautious behavior. The life he has made for himself excludes them and he feels so much better about himself as he cuts them away and draw to himself loving, kind people.

Rabbi is reaching seventy five years and he is rich, making over $200,000 from his accounting. He receives royalties from his books slowly. His publisher says that someday some big publishing house will catch onto his books and offer him large amounts. It almost does not interest him. He shares his money with all those surrounding him. Some are grateful, some not. He saves no money and he trusts in his god to protect him and that god has always protected him. He has long term health insurance to someday be put in a nursing home. He is so fortunate and thankful for all he has. Rabbi was so fortunate to be able to love Patricia for over thirty-five years. He needed someone to love and she died and he never looked back at all he did for her and her husband. Their lack of being grateful was never an issue. His sister and Leroy being ungrateful is not an issue. The only issue was that he was as kind and generous as he could be under god's laws. That is what makes him feel good about himself. He did the best he could and gave what he could of love to others.

Most all of his family members are as I have just described.

Rabbi wanted two of his sisters to know, Gene and Athena, that he has learned that they are not like his other family. They are kind and generous people who value their friends out of loyalty and make a peaceful life for themselves since the loss of their husbands.

If anything came out of Rabbi's short exposure to his family at that party, it was the increase of feelings for the two widows, as has come to a deeper love for both of them.

"Thank you for being so different. Although there are a few exceptions to my family's attributes, such as Roger and Karen Matthews and very few others, you: Gene and Athena are the gems in my mental composite of love. Thank youl." he said.

Chapter Thirty Three

Rabbi Pitches A Bitch

Shopping Carts – For the people who leave their empty carts in or near the parking spaces, we will incarcerate them and force them to bump into things on the way to the mess hall.

Tail-gaiters – For the people who drive too close, we will install hoses with paint to spray their cars.

First-in-line rushers – For the people who speed up to get next spot in the check-out line, we will wait till they get in front of us, then we will spill oil near their feet.

Cut-in-and-out drivers – For the erratic drivers who switch lanes constantly, we will get the hell out of their way since no matter how much we drive safely, they will do what they do to all the people ahead of us.

To the bug eradicator trucks – We will roll our window down and yell to them, "Hey, you got a bug on your windshield. "
To the people who stop far over the painted line, we will yell at them, "Use your kids coloring book to stay within the lines. "
To the people who leave perishable rejects in the tissue aisle, we will bump into them with our buggy.

Chapter Thirty Four

Rabbi Talks About His Daughter

I do not write to accuse. I am a writer and poet, and I write to uncover what truth lies below the surface of things. All my life I have been an introspective person who has remained independent of ordinary concerns. Being a loner compensates for itself by my inquisitive nature leading me far-and-afield into areas that I could never imagine.

To Whom It May Concern is written to a person who has been afraid to interact with me. A person that I love very much.

The first fifteen years of our relationship were filled with love. The next eighteen years also were filled with love. There was a demarcation event in between that lay heavy on your's and my heart, but it was not as important an event to cause problems. That event has proven immaterial over time because it was surrounded by years and years of love.

You changed after thirty five years. You changed professions and attained credentials by your hard working nature. When that level of attainment arrived you made a choice to sever yourself from the past and attach yourself to someone else exclusively. In order to become "exclusive" with that person, you lowered your standards and made yourself into a victim to coincide with your new mate. He considered himself a victim and you became a self-imposed victim with him. Basically you situated yourself socially to cut yourself off from the ones you loved. Your family then even deserted you as the most severe consequence of your actions.

You, like everyone in the world, have the right to create your experience as a learning platform from which you will grow. Whether you did or did not do the right thing is irrelevant. What is relevant is what you take from your situation as time continues.

I have informed you and reiterate so here, that I will never stop loving you in all of its implications. That will never change. My love is expressed in legal documents and here in writing forever.

Chapter Thirty Five

Rabbi Gets Silly Poetic

Beans with bacon
Tea for two
I am so happy
being a Jew

I lead the field of
Christian saints
being Muslim
I ain't

I switch religions
I am sure
Buddhism
is my cure

Remember once
heaven closes
I am coming back
bringing roses
I cook slowly
Eat so quick
I sleep and that's
my bailiwick

I am not a victim
I spit at fate
I laugh at doctors
who berate

Conservatism
washes thin
I live radically

I always win

I will be punished
for bragging
But, that's too bad
So stop nagging

I never take things
serious
I never do things
injurious

I am a fool
I eat grass
my name is
Thom-ass

Chapter Thirty Six

Everything New - A poem by Rabbi

come sing me a sparrow's sadness tree limb hovel of anguish
let loose the drama rattling around the hollows of your heart
tenderness settles itself over vibrations of tears and mistrust
allow chorus's cover to last long into echoes of ministrations
we wait limbo's shadowed entrances spilling themselves blue
ointments of vicarious messages fill up the caverns of night
I remember your innocent ribbon banners flagged in light
you have lost no glamour as excitement surrounds pieces of you
worthiness puffs into all you give to the world of grace and love
heart's left over delicacies sandwiched between sorrows
lay down beside spent passion of eyes closed in trust
we will outlast the days and begin again forgotten

Chapter Thirty Seven

Anna And Anthony

Along the white dusted chalky road crooked posts of weathered wood marked the path. The uneven slant of walkway veered erratically disappearing where the land fell below the blue sky. Anna felt the sun down her neck where she loosened the string tie of her blouse. The canvas pack of mint, spice bush pickings and clover for the evening salad swung against her side as she strode along. She saw the vineyards coming into view where his family and hers were famous for their grape vines twisting their knurled patterns in twines of close fit growth over canopies like thatched huts.

He was a curious man. Except that his curiosity never led him to tasks that the others took up in the village. Anna kicked a stone and made a silent curse under her breath. She had no fantasy idea of what type of man he was. He lived in Thusula, the small clearing of houses along the slope of Mount Sannine. He was her age and was schooled, like her, in the town but his mind was elsewhere. She knew it. She did not like him. He was empty. He had no heart. She would talk to Lewis, her brother, about him and they both would arrive at the same conclusion: Anthony hated the mountains and could not wait to leave. He wanted no part of grape vineyards, sheep and backwards peoples who had no idea what lay outside their towns.

Anthony had been born in the Panama Canal where he lived till his father died of Malaria. His mother brought him back to the mountains but the mountains never welcomed him back.

Anna was the envy of all the girls in the village since Anthony was their dream of the most handsome man to marry. Anthony had deep brown eyes with a green layer to them. He was a big man with fingers twice the size of others. His father had huge hands. His father died digging with so many other men to carve the land open for the canal to flow. Anthony wanted no part of working like his father. "You are a rich boy. " His mother would tell him. "Our family owns all the grape vines in the mountains. " To him, being rich was being unhappy since he wanted only a car, cigarettes, music, dancing and a life of having fun. Being forced to marry Anna, seemed like a way out of the village since the marriage came with a dowry that would allow him to take Anna to the new world – to Detroit where other people of his village had gone.

"Anthony, you are lucky. Anna can make soap and cook. " He looked past his friend and saw emptiness.

Section Two

* New Poems *

On Viewless Wings

(Great Horned Owl, Bubo virginianus)

To those of you who see this page of words
And balk at length and depth of studiousness
Better that you watch TV or join the herds
Of easy reads or sports enthusiasts
For mysteries of nature come so rare
As speckled stars that follow shooting streaks
Moons that hover about a veiled mist
Planets Red shift glare
The blanking blue dissolved sky to peaks
Of vacant spaces where Gods hold tryst

Oh!   But stay to hear the city stopped
Within its houses, parks and sleepy streets
The singularity nocturne hooted popped
Speckled, ear tufted hunter of prey treats
Who eat with no such dainty finesse
Nor cough quiet, snore, or pray aloud
To gods who hear all that is said
Destruction of nests
Justice abstained from being justly proud
To render judgments to the pointless dead

The fierce ripping by talons on a strike
Blood, tendrils sliced with no concern
The blind hunger, tormented thirst like
Desert's notorious suns of fierce burn
Perceptions of holiness crowded with war
This creature would feign to abjure
The cowl or miter - coverings ideal
Nor stop to implore
Mendicate a ravage for a cure

Trade its riches poor for a meal

Lo, whilst soundly earth and I slept
Through walls, thin windows came a call
Shaking the soul. resonance of depth
Subterranean sentimental echoes crawl
Ho-ho-hoo hoo hoo
Curtailing dreams not like an ancient crow
Nor the fibrous shriek of an eagle's catch
Ho-ho (We knew)
Fibrous, sooth, silentious and slow
"Pair Calling" eternity seeking a match

What is this sound familiar on recollect
Robed and cold I tense in March frigidity
Motionless aviary on branch I detect
In charcoal semblance close to me
Back I remember a forest deep
When woken to this owl language
I t was my mother's mom spirit strong
"Hooing" me from sleep
Divesting me of fear of human baggage
Spelling me to dreams of ancient song

Birds wake us drowsy to morning bright
Parrots dazzle the drain of color schemes
Finches and sparrows swallow our sight
Former hawks of terror dredge our dreams
Never has erric falsetto wooed the weak
Stricken the orators of speech, sans tongue
Or suspended bluest angels in their choirs
But the horned speak
Of tufted authority of great owls sprung
From the supreme silence of dead fires

Close your eyes when this bird cries
Pledge your innocence to the forest gone
Cross your heart to ancestral ties
Give hope to resilience of nature's pawn
For here is the centrifuge of creation
The rib taken from the burst of planets
Yes, the black dawn
The great horned owl of summation
Mesmer of ho-ho-ho dramatics

And bet your boots, remain totally still
Night is wary of the progress of evolution
For the life of many is the memory of the kill
The hope of the future is tempered dilution

We give ourselves as bait for higher powers
To forge the banners of demands in time
Expulsed forgotten over a horizon
of secret towers
where issue sounds that chime
the howl of the owl denizen

I Try Hard At Patience Toward Ignorance.

Being kind to the unwary fool
Is my most delicate balance
since I am more than often
them by displacement.

Lone Poem

No matter how things turn out
As in all my efforts to rhyme.
My voice is less than a shout
Words worth less than a dime.
Sad singer of sad sorrow
Alone in questioned state.
No heart to beg or borrow
A pilgrim without a plate.
The cat outside my window
Cries a ghost back to life.
Dead weight a devil in tow
Like a man without a wife.
But time plays it's big joke
And love just might grow
Inside my heart awoke
In your smile eyes aglow.

Forsaken

Damned innocence cloaking love blind
Spread thin over unwary hearts of trust.
Dissuading desire from cautions kind
Encouraging dark reality burning lust.

Oh! The touch of skin, kiss of fire
Couples moaning, eyes closed to light.
Sweet taste of sweat, passion desire
Clouding over sense of wrong-from-right

Thus asleep dust whispering angels tell
Wind to waken curtain windows wide.
Sleepless walls to close out nights spell
And show tableau of what lovers hide.

How we oft turn and run to truth
Forsaking deeds a devil does forsooth
But hope tempestuous like a fire-cloud hove
I' the other's gaze, even as in his whose wand

Vainly all night with spell-wrought power has spann'd
The unyielding caves of some deep treasure-trove.
Also his lips, two writhen flakes of flame,
Made moan: "Alas O Love, thus leashed with me!

Wing-footed thou, wing-shouldered, once born free:
And I, thy cowering self, in chains grown tame,—
Bound to thy body and soul, named with thy name,—
Life's iron heart, even Love's Fatality. "

Life

I write because I have to
There's no other way out
Life presents itself to do
What's right and never pout

What's wrong is to be unkind
When others break the rules
You try to pay them no mind
For ignorance has no clues

A fool can be an asshole
Speaks in forked tongue
Their egos are a grass full
Of snakes hid among-

Among a desert rain
Collected into pools
Along barren terrain
Dust spiraled spools

Elastic night besides
Silted Silver moons
Lizards shed hides
Wind whisper dunes

I forgive, try to forget
My pain won't erase
Devils from my heart
Dark from my face

Life is never black or white
Experience teaches us to wish
For peace and never to fight
For to love is to live in bliss

Being Reborn

When I awake to a new morning, I feel reborn.
It takes a bit of time for my eyes to clear
  as well as my mind getting focused.
I know that re-birthing happens
  in several manners:
Letting a preacher dip your head
as a congregation sings
Letting a doctor tell you your test results
I felt so reborn after my divorce.
I had thought of changing my name out of celebration.
I get the feeling of being new
when I pay off a credit card in full.
If my gas gauge reads empty
and I make it home safe, I breath a relief.
One of the most important times to be reborn
is after a great meal with a small glass of wine.
I will tell you the most vivid time I was born again
was when the mortar rounds stopped falling and,
 amid all the dead bodies, I was still alive.

New Year's Poem

Calm pervades
Eyes screen gray semblances
Fingers loosen thinned threads of emptiness

It was only yesterday that I loved you
I am resigned to your disappearance
In little cubes of thoughts, you sifted between
the rocks gathered in stillness

Here is where your breath left a vapor on my neck
Here a sense of your body wilted to garlands of aching
Why did the excitement of you become so lonely

I will change the dates of forgetting
Before angels entangle themselves in sleep
I will become a spirit of forgiveness,
taking away what pain is left over
and wish you a new year built upon
so many yesterdays of love

I Wonder

So many nights
before morning comes
Laying breathless
in sleepless agitation
I hear a voice and it is not yours
or any person I know, so I pray:
Take away my sight since I am alone
and do not need to see
Give me a weight to lay heavy on my soul since
I am a sinner
So many nights
before the day begins
I wonder where is peace in my heart
and do I have to die to finally rest in your arms.
Take away my hearing because
I need silence to cover me over.

Take away the time because it is worthless to me
to feel the minutes
or feel the uselessness of words of comfort.
Take away the hours.

I wonder if you have doubts
and do you cry for comfort.

I am not blessed nor do I mourn for comfort
I wonder why do you allow me to feel pain
that I did not cause or wish for.
So, I wonder and I wish
for a different lesson to come to me

I wonder where is my friend - sleep
Where is that angel that dusts my eyes drowsy
Where is that force of peace that gives me comfort.

A Chant Poem

my presence is perchance neither here nor there
in time
for I am howabalita no mo freestray
la la la la la la la la
moshasha sho drapoala
du pre da pray made
muntro mundi my heart lets you into its chambers

so ho padatra mdua matro
mun u shor ma mati
shianti mungula pardeeeeeee
shama shuma ma ha putre

ungggggggggggggggg
matra
deeee
propa noti
mata junga do lasee
procee u we shwee

let the slow sound of chant
take me to stray lands of mystery

puptu matri
undo la la la la la la la la la la

soda sostria padu prayu
sogot pro naryee no most per day

I am lost in the purdu paya
I am shut out by shuti nyra nu

sad among the mongo shiva sat suranday

Ancient Lore

I come across time ticking
Molecules humming against the stillness
A beehive of invisible whispering

Less the world forget itself in sleepiness
Awake in loneliness
Like the blink of a bat upside-down
Or the "pair-calling" of the owl,
echoing across centuries

I recall ponds alive with frogs and peepers suspended
above loon's choral, silver night shadows

The distance from branch to water
as the kingfisher dives

Oh! And the surprised croak of the grouse
coming out of the wet weeds of bulrush
flailing themselves to a secret wind

There were the chirp of dozing tree birds
dreaming safely behind leaf cover
and the famous sweep of hawk wing
plunging with hunger driven talons

I love this world within worlds –
page-by-page volumes of ancient lore

Heaven

Maybe there is a heaven. If there is, I can only imagine the reward for people. I call it a reward, but it could well be a punishment. We tend to refrain from bad language when someone does us a discourtesy. We are so careful to be sure that we are not criticizing something we are guilty of. It would be hard to see myself rushing to get ahead of others in line. The faces of brutish people ignore looking at surrounding grimaces as they hurry up and push ahead as if they were on a critical mission. We do silently say to ourselves: "Bastard". But we never speak it aloud. I have a secret wish for a laser pistol that makes people disappear, if they offend me. But, I know that all my relatives and social group on the other side of the veil, would hate it if I sent jerks to them. Out of courtesy, I would laser a few nice people so as to please my ancestors. It isn't as if my relatives are perfect. I would laser Uncle Joe on the other side and send him back to earth. Joe was a very weak man with a face of a dissolute savage. He had a terribly twisted nose and ear from the gangsters beating him up for not paying his bets. My uncle had a rancid smell. It was a deep fragrance of mold like where worms live. I could well imagine him on a hook as bait for whales.

We would have to attach his brother Tony on multiple splitter lines for trawling. The two brothers were reprehensible. They were thieves. They spoke out of turn and never spoke of anything important. They both would remind people of what little favor they gave as a continual hope for hand-outs.

I Wanna Be With You

Wanna find you in the fingers of strings of suns
reflecting off of rivers flowing into the night.

Follow you down the streams of silence
as they travel from the slips of dripping
waterfalls of golden sparkles like eyes
of smooth airless droplets of water.

Take me through the forest
and let me loose in lakes and oceans.
Take me through the plains of dryness
and creature's footprints.
Bless me with your graces like little dreams
of moist pools.

Find me with you
in dew morning mentioned lips of hunger.
There is blood in my eyes. There is salt in my tears.
There are halos saintly around my heart
of yearning for you.
I call to the wolf of mystery.
I wait for the hidden eyes
half mad in the misty lagoons of leaves
and shadows.

I come up for air with my sins let go
into the river Jordan.
I let go of all my hopes with one touch of your fingers.
I wanna go to whoever is left to feel or remaining after
all others have disappeared into the layers of rocks.

Come with me to the little lakes of loneliness
and we will dip into the chemistry of salvation.

The Cat Without A Christmas

I will tell you a cat of Christian
faith known a cusp of Christmas
found scrapping near dumpsters
singing choral "inspiritus" cheers.

Never to tell its faithless roots
Abandoned by saints and crooks.

Stare, you might, out-stare its eye
Never blink though blink you try
For it is in the zone beyond us
Where devotees don't discuss.

Soul, it has with no fixation
To church or school tradition.

This cat with no name or religion
Sometimes snatches a loose pigeon.
No mercy is ever extended
Nor good will ever intended.

We can give it a smile so true
As it is only a cat who knew
How to handle living alone
Without a hearth or home.

To Be A Sunday Worshiper

To be a Sunday worshiper
Whispering silently to God
Woken warm under cover
Sun drench curtains nod

Thankful for breath warm
Wiggle our toes to start
Prayer begins a swarm
Of wonders in our heart

The cell phone vibrates
We fix coffee in a pot
Infused odor insinuates
Joys we never forgot

Cathedral kitchen offers
Hymnals of silent type
Condiments in coffers
Curse but never gripe

Back to bed to sleep
Day can hold a place
Our yawns go deep
Sleep sins all erase

Light That Has Survived

Throw thyself - cold ice will not free sacrifice
nor follow your intentions to hellish paradise.
You are but a grief-ridden sod of sodomite,
A layer of leaf bleached-brief vacant erudite.

Suns of sorrow, bitter tastes of moon's wake
How little we grow with less than we can take.
But fear not, thy velvet cloak of invisibility
will strip away pretension taking any purity.

How salvation depends upon lasting mercies
when fear silences disgust in small travesties.
There is the road left open by wishing the best
and march, we do, toward all we do so detest.

We are leaving an earth better than we arrived:
Breathless gestures of light that have survived.

History

It is beyond our imagination that history is within our perspective. History unfolds the magnitude of horror of war and its effect. We cannot comprehend the scope of suffering to peoples. We read and try to understand what forces unleash death.

If murder is so rampant in history, how do we count resurgence. There can only be one avenue of human population - reincarnation. Our humankind deaths pale in comparison to our human populations. There is no justification for war's injustice to civilian populations.

The intensity of population growth is a force against human suffering. There are now more people on the earth than ever has been in history. We have reached an demarcation point of not having enough food.

As a writer and poet, I can only draw one conclusion to history: We cleanse ourselves by attrition in wars and natural disasters. And, in the process, historically, there is no distinction between civilians and soldiers. We are one in growth and one in death.

My Success Becomes My Failure

When a person sells themselves to another person
or gives themselves over totally to an idea or belief
then they become "self-less" in the true sense.
They no longer have a "self-image" to cling to.
They no longer are a person in control of themselves.
They become a puppet to their ideology.
They forgo their right to their own soul.
They cannot write or speak honestly,
or act as an individual.

All their actions revolve around pleasing
their indenture.
They are fixed like an addict to the object
of their slavery.
They know it. They are so obvious yet oblivious.
The heart of an empty person is a black vessel.
Their heart is no longer filled with charitable deeds.
I do not judge. I only report what I see as a poet.
I will not be part of any group
or accept points from anyone.

I hold my own contests from my own points.
I judge my contests as impartially as possible.
Do not get me wrong - I am still an asshole idiot.
I try so hard to rise above my inanity
And, if I say I succeed, then I have failed.

You Three Times Love

night in your eyes asleep
crickets awake to my ears
tomorrow waiting restless

summer alive by frog call
serenading a full house moon
to a heart emptying a loneliness

Autumn blooming
fanfares of flowers afire
color of your eyes of desire

We Were

follow the forest edge
where we slept nights away
there was honor to our feelings
an honesty of touches
then the trees came to an end
an ocean swallowed us whole
and spat us out into emptiness
in the morning we were forgotten

The Peacemakers

Crying wounded in a wilderness of solitude.
Tears for history confounded by mayhem.
Torn life from all pages of decency as the
cat left in the rubble of orphans alone.
I have seen bullets
come out the other side of surprise.
Shrapnel leaving holes
in the hearts of innocence where
light of an errant god shines aimlessly into night.
No longer do we trust Robert Schumann's fantasie:
"Langsam Getragen: Durchweg Leise Zu Halten"
Please forgive me from romanticism
such as blessed are the wishes of the peacemakers
for they shall be nailed to the wall of destiny.
We all will go to our death in deprivation.
There will be no
"Flights of angels sing thee to thy rest!
And why does the drum come hither?" –
For sweet repose
to blot out the memory of Priam
or the pain of Achilles.
Take the tablets from Sinai.
Turn them into dead sea scrolls
that cannot be read for fear of reprisals.
The lord speaks
through the mouths of wayward elders
who have no faith.
Like children whose voice is lost amidst the tracer fire,
we are the peacemakers who walk blind into napalm.

Beatitude Of Mercy

It takes a lot of trouble to be a poet.
One has to spin the world a ball-bearing.
Smote the wind with northern whimsy.
Single out hawk's cry from trees sowing.
Bring out heaviness, cure it, reinvent.

I lack luster to shimmer oceans.
Have not strength of rooted oaks.
Pale beside Autumn's technicalities.

There was a chemist extraordinary.
His potion killed the one he loved.
But, she became perfect for the grave.
He became perfect for regret.
That's poetry, like Patroclus's envy.

I carry the burden of history
in dungeons of despair.

I live again for Christian ontology.

Impressions of heroes wax thin.
I never tell those I admire
for fear they will dissolve.

My cave of isolation
immures me captive.

Love pours forth from my chakras.
Recipients never are asked returns.
Why would one ask the moon mercy?

River Eyes

skies grey down drizzle asphalt rivers bend
my eyes blur tunnels spiraling never to end
surely our homes are dissolved by all dread
but hear sparrow's sorrow song's joy instead
colors burnt coils within leafless trees spent
rivers tear themselves till death must repent

Precious Memories

precious memories

lay in lacquer
on scales
of time
keep
me

beautiful listen
to unseen birds
hidden in song
from our eyes

when all is lost
all is found
in favor
of our
eyes

travel two roads
leave ourselves
between worlds
spiral into edges
of fruit so sweet
no god can deny
how hard we try
to be better off
than before we
started singing
mandolin sparks
joy within us

precious sacred
little space of love
splintered to gold
embers of echoes
we are given rest
among the boughs
of silver branches
with those birds
father's feathers
hide us safely
in precious

Forsaken

Damned innocence cloaking love blind
Spread thin over unwary hearts of trust.
Dissuading desire from cautions kind
Encouraging dark reality burning lust.

Oh! The touch of skin, kiss of fire
Couples moaning, eyes closed to light.
Sweet taste of sweat, passion desire
Clouding over sense of wrong-from-right

Thus asleep dust whispering angels tell
Wind to waken curtain windows wide.
Sleepless walls to close out night's spell
And show tableau of what lovers hide.

How we oft turn and run from truth
Forsaking deeds a devil does forsooth

File Me Away

All poets rise above the soup of ordinary.
Scan library's shelves of wonderment
and we are insignificant in scale like
constant freeway traffic or that slow
up-down of persistent suns taking
their cue from their solar gods.

All poets trust in their recognition
by invisible forces that brought
them into existence and will
waste them away to death's
inexorable time degradation.

All poets see the folly of ego
and mock the shallow kind.

The words of poets in their finery
dressed like prim-and-proper
adornment, taking imagery
to the highest level of their
imaginations - these words
are vain attempts to describe
what can only be felt - these
words that add to creation's
further elaboration of reality.

I am face-down humble to
even be called a poet.
I always wait for the shoe to fall upon me,
or the voice out of the clouds denouncing
me as a fake, making me tremble in shame.

Waiting

Well, I am waiting around this heaven
Waiting for some magic to place
Within the bosom of everlasting.

I am tired of trying to chase the devil
Out of my heart of wariness.
I am waiting for a message
Like Ezekiel in the desert

Seeing faces in the sand.
I am medly electric.
Suspended chant.
Train conductor-less.
Shiftless ship-less captain-less.

My hope is diminished by all the pain
of worldly craziness.
Even in my solace I worry about the
danger of radicalization.
So, I pray -

Jesus you are my rock and roll.
Jesus you are my conductor.
Jesus you are my engineer.
Buddha you bring me to quietness.

Confucius you teach me to love my neighbor.
I am waiting around the bus station.
I am waiting around the airport.
I have a ticket to salvation and
I am bringing you along with me.

Yea! The two of us will pass through
the veil of innocence
And enter the portals of Valhalla
where all the gods will welcome us.

Even as I write at the best,

I am the worst.

You, my poet friend, are my judge.
I sing to you like a bird of unconscious.
I bail you out of obscurity by my presence.
I furnish you with a benchmark of status.

Label me, staple me, file me away in your memory.

Fire Of My Soul

"Sky above me - Earth below me - Fire within me" –
A Viking Saying

Somewhere; Between A Star

And Air I Breathe

I leave a slipstream for you to follow me.
Limits of my arms becoming wings constrain me.
You are my star reaching to rise me above the world.

I sink below the permafrost in hibernation.
My soul is tired and rests in silence with you
guarding me.

Here in the emptiness of sleep
there is eternal life within me
as a kindle of hope that aspires to be born
over-and-over.
Like the earth,
I have a core fire remaining from my creation.
It is the magnet of what binds me to you in similarity.
It is my soul lit forever i
n unison with an invisible force.

Religions

Five hundred fifty five ways to see god
I give a penny for each, they take back two
The dealer sweeps my bets off the table
And I walk away swearing never to come back

Two Minute Warning - Fourth And Goal

Time collects in back slaps of camera dizzy seconds.
Little did we know the immediacy of
ex-spouses or enemies
of valor-less sympathies.
The neighbor we avoided lines up against us.

Weather is bad. History is silent in the doorway
to death.
There are no previews or special last minute heroics.

Erase the childhood hope for redemption.
Our mother is not here to defend us.

I remember how climbing had temporary
resting camps
as the wind tore the flaps of our tents open
like some invisible god was angry
at our achievements.

Each morning we moved up with renewed hope.
But now there is no precipice above us.
Thunderbolts split the air.
Rain and snow pelt us.

We exchange glances;
Shut out all meaningless prayer.
It is only ourselves that we face as the veil splits open
leaving ragged ends of scrolls with their ink dripping
into the crevices of our eyes
waiting for a desert to dry.

Blood Test

She loves me, she loves herself, keep it to yourself.
Love is fickle and she is as capricious as an elf.
Tomorrow will find her eating at another plate,
Today we find her posing for a picture on a date.

Ah! The apple does not fall far from the tree.
Men picking up her dress, see what they see.
A whole lot of trouble comes from innocence,
Forsaking wisdom on our knees in penance.

But, big the game, so small the just rewards,
Enter jungle wild as lions, leave as cowards.
We men will boast holding up joyous cheer,
But, her parents will pull us off by our hair.

The family conspires to have us gone.
The doctor joins us, our genes belong.

Displacement

When I am in a crowd I remember my hatred
of being crowded
into association of closeness with people
who are uncomfortable

with solitude of emptiness
where all conversation is unnecessary.

Overly touchy souls who seek
not to know underlying realities
portraying false self-confidence
as if their presence is sufficient
to overcome the intimacy of
the savage poet's observances.
Having my sun sign in the
twelfth house of the Babylonian system,
I prefer being alone as
the most efficient way to serve others.
My preference for quiet extends itself
out to expanses of lonely deserts
or that restful space between star groups.

I learned to enjoy cafeterias
where the noise of discussions allowed me
to not single out any one voice
but the unhindered avenues of nothingness;
so easy to lose myself within in thought.

If you were to compare me to
the wary beast cautious for danger
or the tiny rodent who can
single out any impending enemy,
then selecting the one animal
for me would have to include
all creatures who protect themselves by exclusion.

Therefore I am a consciousness of specialty
with a soul of distinctness as if self-contained
within an ego that displaces definitions
for extreme self-preservation of forever.

The Rabbi Prays

For the night wind spaced between heaven's scent,
Wherever you are Adonai I am with you in spirit.
Out of the stretched silences of the dark desert sands
silted through their shifting elements, I bless you,

Here in the vacancy of my heart
I wait for your presence
to fill me with healing ointments of empathy
and wisdom.
My Adonai who sends all emissaries of angels
to tend to me.
My Adonai who collects me into patient corners
of ease.

Baruch atah Adonai elohaynu melech ha'olam asher
kidshanu bemitzvotav vetzivanu l'hadlik
ner shel Shabbat.
When the stars bring light to my eyes,
it is you I see Adonai
When the spilling of emptiness covers the heavens,
it is you.

Out of the fear of my insecurities
I seek your guidance.
In my humble way of restraint
I trust in your protection.
My Lord of differences
who subjects me to the particular
I select the finest words that will please your ears
and speak them on paper to you with music
of the wistful sounds.

My Lady god of mixtures who is my Adonai angel,
I swear to allegiance of your mysteries.

My Adonai of woman magic's, please grant
me the grace of your thoughts forever.

I am never sure of my homages.
I am always in debt to your gifts.
I begin and continue with your aid.
My Adonai of angels who dusts my eyes
with desert soil
I pray in simple presence of your elixir of aperitif.

You are the after echo of snow fall
across the glacial connections
entwined between mountains
in blue specter ice.

I am the whisper of syntactical psalms.
Hear me Oh lady of mercies.
Bless me with gold amber
shadows of evenings dew.

Our Gentle Hearts Throb With Praying

Tis not the dead that speak of living
It's us that need the act of forgiving

Life returns in circles of unknowing
All futures depend on who is giving

Bestir thyself with hope in deriving
The memory of our souls arriving

Oh! Sweat of humanities striving
For equanimity's newest devising

Lay hate to rest, pick up appraising
Our gentle hearts throb with praying

Less words, more silence in saying
That peace within us never delaying
The object in life is to live weighing
What death means for us surviving

Awakening to Hope

It is far too early to judge humanity
Collectively dissolved in blood
True-or-false in intentions Indiscernible by immersion
Into a wish-wash of sunsets.

By weight of charity versus hate
Various histories lie still as stone
And no epithet suitable devised.
It is a compilation of feather-fall sandwiched
between glaciers.

Certainly confounded Blindly in a balance
of confidence in justice.

The swing factor toward ablution
Is a faint breath of Eve expiring
By degrees favorable in poetics.

Hear a whisper of silence
winning over as planets subside.
It is always only kindness
that awakens our hearts to hope.

It's Only A Miracle

daddy is dead and mamma is waiting her turn
there is moisture coming from their eyes
like tears wetting the linen of dead mummies
I noticed the emptiness without them guiding me
I am here in the dark
and watching their mystery dissolve
there is very little left but emptiness of light
we all go to the same place upon dying,
the sacred rooms of sleepiness
I would rather be alone
as the world keeps it's pace
seems like our insecurities get set aside
and we carry our privacy into the grave
there is a whole lot more to welcome us
across the veil
it's only a miracle
and we take it for granted
as the crying of the souls
covers over our fears
it's only a miracle
and we collect stars
before the morning comes to welcome us

Being So Mean

sometimes empty
sometimes clean
longing for someone
not so mean

days without sun
nights with no one
longing for a queen
not so mean

remember tomorrow
was same as today
we grew up different
not so mean

time is a mountain
piled high in dreams
see everything below
keeping us above
being so mean

sadness is blessing
making us wiser
charity is our lesson
helping us rise above
being so mean

often I am alone
never lonely
you are my prayer
my earthly angel
never mean

Vastness

There have been times when things stopped around me. Like, totally stopped. I paused to sense what was happening and briefly closed my eyes. Deep in the recesses of some part of me that remains hidden, most all the time, a reverberation of stillness hums as an electrical disconnect.

It is uncanny, to say the least. It is an opening to a layer of reality as in an unexplored vacuum that can be frozen then come back to life thawed bit-by-bit in a dynamic balance of wordless containment.

This "State Of Awareness" is depth-less in shadows of silver oracles. I can become part of this entrapment as long as I do not try to control it. I must let the pillow of content hold me within its mystery. I must give up all thought and allow the ambiance of this query become a part of me immersed within this wolf stare of becoming.

I have experienced this phenomena in instantaneous crisis when I was held between worlds in emergencies such as car accidents or within the bellows of warfare during exploding shells and death surrounding me in an exhale of bombastic silences.

A force of gentleness emerges during these hiatuses. A force so spiritual that engulfs my heart with precious love so healing in its confluence.

It is a love not part of time or motion. It is a love of feeling free to want all that can be given in a way that I want only to give back what is given to me.

In this state of profundity I glaciate into bluish clarity. I become, as if, emptied of myself and inhabiting an unknown persona. It is beyond elevation or geometric spaciousness. I feel like a sojourner or pilgrim of a vastness breathless in its scope.

Your Smile A Salvation

Immobile in somber death forgot
You lay as warriors bloated bier
Eyes closed, scant breathing
Imploded in secret dreams

My fear is you are forsaken
By derelict gods out of fashion
Intransigent angels black burnt
By cold fires of hell's constraint

A mockery of your savage tongue
In days past your vitriol scathing
Against featherless vagabonds
Deserving not your benedictions

All gone beside dried ocean streams
Of fish boned deserts skin shriveled
To whorled sand storms desiccation
Adventure-less you sleep infamous

My tears collect by indifference
My prayers die at their roots
I wipe your forehead sweat brow
And give you my best last rites

The tree has severed roots
The earth replaces itself
My memory keeps laughing
With your smile a salvation

Starting All Over

Our grandfathers are farther away
Than our ancestors here today
They hear our yearnings
And all we think or say

We are linked back to the ape,
Small or large creatures who gape
Into the star splintered sky of night
That we wonder at with such delight

The world around us is wrought
With hope we paid for or fought
Till our bloodless bones condensed
Into soiled ice cave's mysteries end

Poetry is just another nature's joke
Ridding us of comedy that we poke
At the sliding wake of humanity
Here or just going up in smoke

Many religions hold us in sway
As we kneel, bow our heads to pray
But we do not give up till we die
Then start over all the things we try

War

At the start it was fun as a young man's fantasy of adventure. Like high school sports recognition for the exceptional - war was the giving back for family members who returned from Europe World War II, with a sense of pride.

The delving into the unknown of volunteering for Vietnam without any concept of Asian peoples culture or history. The French being driven out of South East Asia was a "non-sequitur" to the ignorance of us soldiers.

In the orientation room, upon landing in Vietnam, incoming soldiers were given prophylactics and told to keep from having children. No mention was made of fighting conditions or terrain. It amazed me that sex was more important than fighting.

We flew into the isolated army base by helicopter. Our assignments were handed out and each of us established ourselves in the barracks quarters.

Vietnam is an oasis of Asian loveliness with rich green rubber plantations, distant horizons of rice paddy beauty spread like a water-spill into the low areas of the greenish fresh land. Water buffalo stood up to their bellies submerged. Half naked people bent over pulling rice out of the mirrored shimmering puddled surfaces. Figures with sun shield round straw hats looked up as we walked past. We would learn, later, how these people lived without any of the very conveniences we are used to.

Each living hut was occupied by men sorted out by their occupation. All the belly gunners who rode astride the helicopter open doors with their guns on mounts, lived in one barracks. The ground troops, who went out on patrol each

day, lived in another barracks. The army called these small baracks "hooches". The army had a name for everything. I remember how social contact was held in meetings in one particular hooch when men got together and oiled and cleaned their guns. The banter and exchange of firearms took place while they drank and smoked. Everybody on the compound seemed to relish having sidearms strapped on their waist as they walked around all day. It was as if they were cowboys and guns were their self-security.

In another particular hooch it was a regular weekly slide show or movie of all the people that had been killed during the week. Men would relish looking at images of dead boys and soldiers tied up and heads hanging down or shot off. It was the most gruesome unholy thing I ever encountered. It was total barbarism.

There are so many stories in my memory of nights of flares, red tracer bullets leaving a trail of lines where bullets found their targets. I spent one whole year with this fighting and nothing in my life compared to finally flying home to try to forget the noise and mayhem and dead bodies.

Through A Silent Moment He Whispered To Me

Through A Silent Moment He Whispered To Me,
through slanted wind-blown silent waving trees.
I closed my eyes to look inward so I could see
lasting remnants of a day letting-up in degrees.

A piano played Rachmaninoff second movement
of concerto number two in C-Minor, Opus eighteen.
It was a direct line to my god that I felt and heard
music beyond music that opened up my soul.

Nothing remained in residue of anxiety or hurt
as each turn of the music swept me away.
Never before had I floated above myself
expanding in an umbrella of light and love.

We are told that being born is much harder
than dying when we follow the fibers holding us.
The wishing for completion is fulfilled
in the deliverance of our hearts out of our body.

Time dissolves. We let go of ourselves into arms
of safety. The succor of our creator heals us.
We are like a module re-fixing ourselves to a core.
We are made to the image and become re-attached.

The highest forces of clarity instill us with gratitude
and we join ancestors of ages, our god-of-all-gods
placing us within the echoes of a faceless whisper.

The Forests of Yesterday

Lonely like sunsets laying across forgotten horizons
Bird singing ended and trees sitting waiting for night
The singular owl being alone for pair calling hoping
Into the hollow tree stump of squirrel havens
Out of the bush of raccoon hunger emerges

These inconsequential creatures spilling out
of nature's scenery not caring for maps or guides.
She left me like a bird who knows where to fly
not caring whether I was sad or glad for her to go.

Between life and love she went quickly away
and the golden grey morning cried with me.
Could I be a beaver and care nothing for dams.
Could I be a hawk and not know how to hunt.

I was a lover who fell out of the net of love
A special person who lost all my specialty.
Keep me from the cold of indifference.
Let me peer out of the hollow tree trunks.

My borders have all been crossed and
My lessons have been turned over in my mind.

Could I have been kinder? Wiser? A little smarter?
All I have left behind are in the forests of yesterday.

Everything New

come sing me a sparrow's sadness
tree limb hovel
of anguish
let loose the drama rattling around
the hollows of your heart
tenderness settles itself over vibrations
of tears and mistrust
allow chorus's cover to last long into
echoes of ministrations

we wait limbo's shadowed entrances
spilling themselves blue
ointments of vicarious messages fill up the
caverns of night
I remember your innocent ribbon banners
flagged in light
you have lost no glamour as excitement
surrounds pieces of you

worthiness puffs into all you give to the world
of grace and love
heart's left over delicacies sandwiched
between sorrows
lay down beside spent passion of eyes closed in trust
we will outlast the days and begin again forgotten

What Was Here

We hear what was gone but came back with melody
of Bach's "Matthew" that comforts us in Christianity.
Later on we are visited by Buddha who approves
of the adulation of his brother who took the pressure
off, and let the world see language of salvation.

There was no reason for you to believe
in the crucifixion
since there were so many zealots
who professed messiah.
Ad agencies of now speak of what was here
for us to believe.
We close our eyes and are led down
a golden path of promises.
Jesus came back from India when
the news spoke of him who was here.

He met with his friends and broke bread for their bodies and gave them words for their souls: "Remember I am with you for all time. Close your eyes and speak my name for I will appear and comfort you with my lasting love. "
The apostles tried passing this down and failed out of dilution of belief. That is: We believe until something else sounds better and allows us to forget the past of "What was there" compared to "What was here" for us to grasp forever.

Jesus And The Blues

Jesus was a lover of the eastern sky
when it shook loose the stars.
Across the Mediterranean he
wished for whales swimming in salt.
He swore to himself to bring
bread to the poor and milk to babies.

His mother hoped he would find
some peace before he got too old.
Jesus watched the fishermen
come to relax and take whores.
He knew the hearts of heaven
would pardon their indiscretions
So, he turned his eyes away
from the laughter, letting day end.

Jesus carried truth in small parts of
his memory to ease his pain.
He never let the swell of ignorance
turn him away from compassion.
Jesus was at home with love.
He felt his best when he pardoned.

It was hard for Jesus because the majority of people,
all of which he loved, were so preoccupied with life
that very few could see the larger picture of God and
all the faith that was lost from their distractions.
We let the lies take us into dark places
and we cry when we lose.

We know that the night will not
cover over our driving desires.
We grow weary asking for forgiveness
so we learn to smile.

When the collision of earth-to-heaven
brings us some sense
Then there is blue in our hearts
and blue in our eyes of love.
Jesus painted the eyes of the world blue
and went to sleep
with blues in his dreams to keep us feeling good
about life.

Red Inside Our Tenuous Lives

Of course, if you are a street person living in the imaginary world of fetid waft rising up, threatening to choke ice cream marble pigeons who cough beneath the acrid veil of shadowed crowded streets, then, and only then, your blood is rinsed by harbor water stench and is grey by indifference to breathing to survive.
Somewhere in the line of evolution, you fit into chaos of civilization whose lack of sewers led to vomit green drippings hanging from rat filled drains. Then your blood was still grey, exactly like today.

I remember begging the whore who walked away from my en-treatments to picnic with me in the country. I pleaded with her to escape before death covered over her nakedness of crushed bread crumb skin. She had the blood of a prisoner of her own war and coughed like the pigeons in phlegm as she threw her fag into the steaming iron metal grill where the street became invisible to the gush of rain washed blood.

Oh, we have all lay beneath the trunk risen tree of chestnut shimmer and felt the clean wind of a park hidden from the city. Here is where our blood was the color of cheap wine staining our lips asleep inside our hearts.

But do not be misled. Those times were crowded into the history of evolution circling itself like a snake around the birth and death of caution.
We knew that there was no other color to blood
but red inside our tenuous lives.

Footprints

I told wind - cover all you can
turbulent reminder of terror
Let there be waves ocean-less
of leaf, limb stormy rage

Remind us of peace
awaiting finality
Whisper to me such of uncovered madness's.
I will make ready places where silence rules
cathedral-like below arched entrances

There the little ones scamper playfully
Here footprints line black river beds
thick in soppy clay evidence
I told wind - tell me of origins
cold avenues thawing into spring canopies
Let me into secret aromatic lilac wishes

Unending Measure

I do not know how or why I loved God, but from my age of reason at five or six, I begin to see the power of creation in all things around me.

My family were indifferent to my fervor.

My friends never understood the clarity with which I feel and know the great spirit force that surrounds us with love and protection.

As a six year old, I simplified my understanding by thinking that all people knew God as I felt God. I prayed every day to the veil that kept God hid from our eyes.

The purity of love through the curtain of time always ends up with God on the invisible levels above and below and around us. The God who keeps us from colliding with disaster is my God. My God creates havoc to some people but, for some reason, not for me.

As a growing human being, I learned to keep secrets of shadows to myself. I learned to keep the mysteries of sound, silence and mistiness quietly inside my soul. I learned that I do have a soul. My soul is the piecemeal composite of all the good things I do for myself and for others. My soul is the growing nodule of sanctity put together like a puzzle inside my heart. My soul vibrates with all the acts of kindness that make up my days of light.

I can only tell you that my soul is made up of all the things I have given up or given to others in my life. I have a soul of gifts. I only give to others, that which I love enough to place in other people's possession. If I give a gift, it is something I love so much and I will only give that gift to others to vibrate in their lives with the love I felt for the gift.

There is no secret to my childhood turning into adulthood. It happens so swiftly and holds itself into place for eternity. My adulthood is my clarity of soulfulness that abides side-by-side with my invisible God that I trust in and love with unending measure.

Papa and The Moon

papa don't crack his bones
hair like white chicken's
bleached eyes sad blue

mama she cares less
than those days gone

papa he laid his gun
against the barn wall
watched for night fall
crossed in shadows

can't tell the difference
tween grey cow patty
from closed back door

papa he turned old
like chipped paint
dusty leaf mold
won't buy more stars
or the sky empties
of all its memories

papa will seal up his time
in his eyes no light arrives.

Alone But Never Lonely

I could be the color of overripe avocados
Adhering to scandals of dark semblances.

I disappear in shadows.

All my lovers reached for me with eyes closed
A camaraderie of soul mates
Flinching at danger
Never deserting.

In moonlight spilled upon
cool Nile banks, I overflowed.

Pyramids rose into place
centuries collected as stones -
My heart hardened
From indifference.

While caravans slept
I enjoined the stars
Silent to a fault.

Have you ever wished for death?
Been rewarded by a full life?

Tomorrow I will return my borrowed eyes.
To scales of justice I concur a balance.

To those who see me, let them lower their voices
And turn aside out of courtesy
To a prejudice of ignorance.

I am alone but never lonely.

Find You Forever

ancients wait for us to come out and teach us
like stories of the fish we never caught
or the mountains we never climbed
they keep us mesmerized by their words

the old rise up from their graves and try to shock us
by their elemental scary visages and grimaces
as they warn of danger or consequences of our acts

sitting on papa's ashes I feel the weight of his world
the dead lie upon us like dirt over our coffin
while we are still alive, they try to smother us

everywhere I look the beauty overwhelms me
the sound of wind and rain soothes me
the wish of trees blowing like wild horses
makes me feel all the distances of time

the old cannot rise up because they are only bones
the past is a remembrance of empty imaginations
it is now that I feel the ice of winter or breath
of spring
the torrents of time tick me to sleep
by crickets singing

I am my brother of generations who wished to be me
I am the last summer of their broken dreams
I am me atop the pile
of evolution sandwiched below me
I am the sweet end of days
and nights of dying sunsets
Cover me over with a thin veil of mist so I can awake
and feel the little joys of fingers
and legs moving aimlessly
I am the spirit of love collecting over you with passion
bringing you to understand how much I find you
forever

Our Burnt Edges

Color me membrane morning mist
Take pigments from ancient skins
Relatives of bones left bleached
Into random swirls red-bled blue
Brought out clean by earth blown
Days reflected pottery brown ocher

Rest upon my hillocks of brush grass
Where deer left their dreams of stars

I am not dead but left to fly free
Atop a tree-line spent in solitude

Weave me embroidered by lace golds
Covering over a Friday feeling of lassitude

I am the tasks of Thursday pinned to a robin's breast
You will hear me whisper-wind tinkle of leaf and limb

Do not look for me but look for ice of constancy
We are frieze waiting of lots
We are the wonder of woven winters
Proving ourselves by patience under
The watchful eyes of so many gods
Who take pleasure in our deeds

We earn the respect of frogs
Atop a floating twig bark

There is green moss in our hearts
Left over happiness in our vapor trails
And tomorrow there will be rain
To take away our burnt edges of pain

A Requiem for the Non-Dead: Prologue

When love ends there is a sadness
When hate ends there is a joy
Love creates a soul piece-by-piece
Hate obliterates a soul
When hate continues, there is no room for recovery
With love there is room for an eternity

All hate is a form of self-deprecation
The object of hate circles back to crush the hater
All the time spent hating is time wasted for loving

All the years spent with love were building years
When you left love in anger those years
lost their value
What hate destroys takes as much time
to rebuild from scratch

The soul is created bit-by-bit
and expands by continued love
I have continuing love for you
Your absence is as if you are dead
So, I can love you through the veil
As if my love for you is a requiem

A Requiem for the Non-Dead; Part 1

First Voice: There is a sadness that escapes past reasoning
Second Voice: Say
First Voice: Like a montage of sorrow lilting as a banner over a sullen sun set
Second Voice: Say
First Voice: I am taken by a voiceless wind into crevices of silence
Second Voice: Say
First Voice: On an echo of past extravagance are less noise and more stretches of nothing

A Requiem for the Non-Dead; Part 2

First Voice Alone: Can you be gay when the sky turns ash brown and a lifeless forest crawls beneath an inescapable cloud

I am always alone by distances. I turn and flowers fade to Fall's foliage.

Come into the room faint-lit and sit among the place-mats of memories.

A Requiem for the Non-Dead; Part 3

The Rich
 Elite constraint of pinnacle propriety
You know:
Spending their inheritance
Lonely in protected estates
But, always,living in abstention.

Didactic
Affrontive
Supercilious
Aloof
Arrogant
Argumentative in the way of absurdity.

Treasures of the rich include
maps of fishing sites long ago dried-up.

The horror of their commandments
are best thrown to pieces and go about
adoring any golden calves available.

You can imagine their expression of relief in organism

as donkeys braying or dinosaurs
with bronchial complications.

But being kind is always a forgiveness
for their conditions.

Always be quiet and never engage them
or you will lose sanity in-the-end.

Praying To The Gods, or

Keeping My Bases Covered

Buddha, by Jesus, I love you to hell
Praying in chants like ringing a bell
I have my direction celled G P S
Turning my life over from a mess

Squared things with ex-spouse-y
Tax man left me empty trouse-y
Beard's gone. My ear ring too
Yarmulke pretending to be Jew

I wear sandals as Mohammad
Bowing to Mecca till I turn red
My heaven is a reincarnation
As a perfect act of contrition

Bless me Confucius for all sin
I confess humbly with a grin

Rhyming has Gone Astray

Humor can only come from minds in total disarray
Sadness is the place when joy has no place to stay
We wish that love not leave but eyes so often stray
Upon green fields lust's absent-mindedness is grey

Our histories remind us life is more than just today
The little worlds we live in confine us in every way
For happiness to remain we must always be gay
Then thoughts of clarity will rule us all the day

We have learned that love is like tooth decay
Plaque of affection builds and won't go away
We brush against each other like sore inlays
Divorces are dismal dramatic morality plays

Oh, it's just fine when we have first parity
Our coupling is an exhaustive fresh party
We fall asleep entwined in a half drowsy
Seen through windows we are propriety

But life draws a string - a necktie
We act out a scene of do-or-die
And each of us pretend to cry

In the end nowhere-or-why
Life is littleness - not big
Marriage is a tree twig
In gardens time digs
New loves from sprigs
in some frond resting place

We Come Apart

We come apart into night's eye
swollen beside a virgin sense
of our nobility of being.

We are fervent in hope.
Forgotten by littleness.
Our life squeezed -
Platelets - condensed -
Leaf scaled into sediment.

There never was a moon
Glistening - on fire with imagination.
It was all so eventful and meaningless.
Do not be fooled by words
because they will fail us in the end.
It is only the sparsity of kindness bolstering
our fears as we slide.

Do not fret the poet's call. It is like the loon crying by the water's edge invisible by darkness but there in essence in some frond resting place.

Ancient Memories

This loveliness of words pauses my breath;
stalls all who read with wondering eyes.
We leave broken icicles of thoughts
in a stream linked by our senses.
Come to the corridors of light
opening hearts to hope.

We are temporary / magnificent
Once beautiful forever timed.
The bones of our celebrations
keep faith in a wind of mercy.
Hear ancestors welcoming us
with tears and bounty joy.
There is never a wrinkle
within ancient memories.

By Death Shall I Conquer -

Per Mortem Vicero

By death shall I conquer
life's many pitfalls.
To hear but allay
pleasure's calls.
The hate, the love
as caution withdraws.
The push and shove,
all reason's flaws.

I am a wise fool
a silent clown;
Experience's tool;
A smile, a frown.
My thoughts outlast
my world's end.
Breaking at last
what desires portend.

See me smile
eyes open wide.
Sincerity's guile
is a loss of pride.

Watch me dissolve
as vapor or mist.
My life will evolve
by sweet tenderness.

For Our Children

Caress softness
Words become real in defense
Imagery bathes the wounds of stench.

"We lay beside each other
Before a wall of death
Stops us from growing
Past our horror"

Blood ran out
Watering a tired soil.

The air received screams
impounding them to hell.
"My mother wherefore art thou?
Return us to the womb blessed. "

Sam collected the dog-tags.
He clamped one inside teeth
and slung the other around his neck.

Sam never got over the terror in the eyes
of the corpses.
He cautioned himself that he was giving final prayer
to his comrades.
"My mother I place myself in your hands
And hope this truly is the last war for our children. "

led in whispers beaten
flickered shadows became so voiceless
lips that broke the solemn morn.

Sun-spattered dreams
in crimson eyes. . . .
Life was life.

Death is death.
Love and roses can answer them.

This place knows such woe
and tends to steep no mercy
as darkness-thick points its finger
the drench of sod in soiled earth

poor souls find no lasting hope
where kingdoms did once pretend.
The soldier's grave
the expense was spent in lonely tomb
largeness comes in solemntude
and my words went very silent:

Each warrior remains in his grave
I pray a rose fills his wilt today.
Nocturne To Love
Evening clings to eyes
Fingers fold to emptiness
Across space dimmed stars salvage
what memories are left waiting for sleep
I am crossed in sanctity by passive breathing

It is all in nodding off to reverie
That calmness of forgetfulness
To put away the day in sachets
A perfumed drained to pillows
Where listing sails fold into night

My last thought is for ancient airs
Of slow streams wilting thinly as
Melodic serenades of Chopin

Close me into you as we meld
Like lovers who were famous
By degrees of drowsiness

Clarity Of Prayer

The secret spell from music that chants me
into reverie.
Vespers of unintelligible languages that
weave mysterious echoes.
Rachmaninoff creates,
as well as Tchaikovsky, choral magic out of sorrow.
Sounds of liquid nectar deepening us
to an inner peace of resignation.
My mother hears and holds me with rocking lullaby's.
My lover falls to silence hovering over me in requiems.
I am suspended in somber moons;
Held by faith in dark heavens;
Calmed by night's sacred stars;
Pulled away from heart-of-sadness;
Solved of life's enigmas by clarity of prayer

Is there anybody out there
Is there anybody out there?
I am being shuttled through a life alone.
All my ex wives have turned off my air supply.
None of my credit cards allow me any extra credit.
I seem to have the largest gas tank on earth when I
fill up.

The charge for my medications
would finance rebuilding the Titanic.
My priest, rabbi and mullah
have rejected my sins as unforgivable.
My blood sugar levels are always
close to putting me into a diabetic shock.
My doctor wants me to explain t
o him why I am so healthy but not yet dead.
If I go on a diet I gain weight. If I eat less I gain
weight. If I eat healthy foods I gain weight.

Every time I change my will, the people I have named or entrusted, desert me including my attorney.
I have holes in all my socks. I wear diapers that keep falling out of my pants when I walk or shop.
I pray every night but never ever get an answer. I have bad dreams with no good books to explain them.
I am an American of Arabic extraction and I have added Buddhism to my Christian and Muslim belief systems.

I have a John Deere seed cap, a New York Yankees baseball cap and a Jewish kippah or yamaka in case Jesus comes back as a farmer, a baseball player or a Jew.

Every one of my favorite poets, writers, philosophers, painters and special people have all committed suicide.

I feel like a fish out of water, I feel like a boat without sails. An engine without any gas. A car with no tires. I pay too much tax. I earn too little money. My budget stretches itself over twenty continents and six planets.

Every check I write bounces off of fifteen satellites and the rotating radar scope on the aircraft carrier Enterprise.

When I finally get to sleep, I wake too early. During the day I fall asleep in my chair or while I am reading.

Oceans

We must have our ocean to see
what is in our hearts to be
in caverns of secret
dim lit sanctuary.

Quite as flagella
motioned by
currents of
swishes.

Waving brushed
to liquid
light.

Our neighbors are schooled
in gentleness and fury
of a landscape
buried in
layers.

Our eternity is above the waves
where a horizon beckons us.
But we stay safe below in
oceans of memories
of silted sandy
bottomless
silence.

Section Three –

Shakespearean Sonnets

Mirrored

Shakespeare Sonnet #1

From fairest creatures we desire increase,
That thereby beauty's rose might never die,
But as the riper should by time decease,
His tender heir might bear his memory:

But thou contracted to thine own bright eyes,
Feed'st thy light's flame with self-substantial fuel,
Making a famine where abundance lies,
Thy self thy foe, to thy sweet self too cruel:

Thou that art now the world's fresh ornament,
And only herald to the gaudy spring,
Within thine own bud buriest thy content,
And, tender churl, mak'st waste in niggarding:

Pity the world, or else this glutton be,
To eat the world's due, by the grave and thee.

Michael Thomas Sonnet #1

All time doth span in ages lost but gives,
to burn to wash on shores of ocean sands.
The sun dries laced the edges of its sieves,
as forests crawl into the cautious lands.

Before our days are many yet to come
across the nights into the vestige wake.
So little touch, so much the ancient drum
where aspirations fade and hearts do quake.

We're now collected cache of all trades,
evened out, and squared, the root of space.
Hold'eth our hands the silver tip of blades
to give who want the mysteries of grace.

I Pity those whom born act as dead.
Wish them well, but gone away instead.

Shakespeare Sonnet #2

When forty winters shall besiege thy brow,
And dig deep trenches in thy beauty's field,
Thy youth's proud livery so gazed on now,
Will be a totter'd weed of small worth held:

Then being asked, where all thy beauty lies,
Where all the treasure of thy lusty days;
To say, within thine own deep sunken eyes,
Were an all-eating shame, and thriftless praise.

How much more praise deserv'd thy beauty's use,
If thou couldst answer 'This fair child of mine
Shall sum my count, and make my old excuse,'
Proving his beauty by succession thine!

This were to be new made when thou art old,
And see thy blood warm when thou feel'st it cold.

Michael Thomas Sonnet #2

It's true that forty years can cause a change
where youth escaped beyond our aged grasp.
Discriminate the lines of brow arrange
so quick our face succumbs to time's elapse.

They who see us say, "How young you look.
I would think you years behind your cat. "
The cover, yet, can not describe the book.
The girth we have is simply baby-fat.

But our ex-spouses always whisper true -
"He" or "she has really gone downhill!"
We can stay the pangs of histories cue
with art, architecture and medicinal pill.

Our memories have such a great release,
money leaves behind us so much peace.

Shakespeare Sonnet #3

Look in thy glass and tell the face thou viewest
Now is the time that face should form another;
Whose fresh repair if now thou not renewest,
Thou dost beguile the world, unbless some mother.

For where is she so fair whose uneared womb
Disdains the tillage of thy husbandry?
Or who is he so fond will be the tomb
Of his self-love, to stop posterity?

Thou art thy mother's glass and she in thee
Calls back the lovely April of her prime;
So thou through windows of thine age shalt see,
Despite of wrinkles, this thy golden time.

But if thou live, remembered not to be,
Die single and thine image dies with thee.

Michael Thomas Sonnet #3

Thine eyes from mirrored out will see
Thy mother's birthing, guiding light
Tender touch of arms encircling thee
As if no harm ever enjoin you in fright

Gesture of acceptance wore patiently
Her dreams quarantined by fact
Burden of responsibility was reality
Fantasy of life was a hidden act

We could see through her thin guise
As she bore down to finish each task
Knowing all giving returned no prize
Peace of mind came, she never asked

All of us, her children, took the gifts
O! Motherhood, its love so uplifts

Shakespeare Sonnet #4

Unthrifty loveliness, why dost thou spend
Upon thy self thy beauty's legacy?
Nature's bequest gives nothing, but doth lend,
And being frank she lends to those are free:

Then, beauteous niggard, why dost thou abuse
The bounteous largess given thee to give?
Profitless usurer, why dost thou use
So great a sum of sums, yet canst not live?

For having traffic with thy self alone,
Thou of thy self thy sweet self dost deceive:
Then how when nature calls thee to be gone,
What acceptable audit canst thou leave?

Thy unused beauty must be tombed with thee,
Which, used, lives th' executor to be.

Michael Thomas Sonnet #4

Appearances facade the waste below
in subtle measure ego slaves the soul
a flower such as wisdom cannot grow
in hostile minds a peace is not a goal

The costume day finds joy alone at night
and truth played-out is often just a ruse
to chase the devil after wrong or right
for mansions shrink inside a bitter house

Though hearth may bear a warmth of kindled need
distraction of these flames may yet fall cold
through self as lonely grasp begone to greed
where lies became a substance freely told.

Mendacity wears garb of subtle grace
worn mask and silhouette a shadowed face.

Shakespeare Sonnet #5

Those hours, that with gentle work did frame
The lovely gaze where every eye doth dwell,
Will play the tyrants to the very same
And that unfair which fairly doth excel;

For never-resting time leads summer on
To hideous winter, and confounds him there;
Sap checked with frost, and lusty leaves quite gone,
Beauty o'er-snowed and bareness everywhere:

Then were not summer's distillation left,
A liquid prisoner pent in walls of glass,
Beauty's effect with beauty were bereft,
Nor it, nor no remembrance what it was:

But flowers distilled, though they with winter meet,
Leese but their show; their substance still lives sweet.

Michael Thomas Sonnet #5

Time covers over our dreams so quick
It helps us forget the season's savor
As summer turns to winter's prick
And spring returns us to its favor

Short the flower forest-floor fern
Laughter recedes a hidden heart
The candle on both ends will burn
As our patience tears pain apart

We are born as marsh marigold
Grown along rakish water edge
Uplifted in yellow stream bold
Giving spring its first pledge

We trust quietly the hand of god
Nature gives us his whisper nod

Shakespeare Sonnet #6

Then let not winter's ragged hand deface,
In thee thy summer, ere thou be distilled:
Make sweet some vial; treasure thou some place
With beauty's treasure ere it be self-killed.

That use is not forbidden usury,
Which happies those that pay the willing loan;
That's for thy self to breed another thee,
Or ten times happier, be it ten for one;

Ten times thy self were happier than thou art,
If ten of thine ten times refigured thee:
Then what could death do if thou shouldst depart,
Leaving thee living in posterity?

Be not self-willed, for thou art much too fair
To be death's conquest and make worms thine heir.

Michael Thomas Sonnet #6

Stay, my mother hair tied back, your face
of expectations long before I cried
out of your deliverances of grace.
Night black, for you, had not yet arrived.

Calm as a stone formed Buddha you swung
from summer, alas, to motherhood so quick
that bells celebrating death were rung
too soon for your flower to be picked.

It's true a river divides us after death
where family, friends wait out our final term.
Expect eternities for one last breath
then face defeat of that bitter worm.

It's in the place where angels seek release
joined with god in league with heaven's peace.

Shakespeare Sonnet #7

Lo! in the orient when the gracious light
Lifts up his burning head, each under eye
Doth homage to his new-appearing sight,
Serving with looks his sacred majesty;

And having climbed the steep-up heavenly hill,
Resembling strong youth in his middle age,
Yet mortal looks adore his beauty still,
Attending on his golden pilgrimage:

But when from highmost pitch, with weary car,
Like feeble age, he reeleth from the day,
The eyes, 'fore duteous, now converted are
From his low tract, and look another way:

So thou, thyself outgoing in thy noon
Unlooked on diest unless thou get a son.

Michael Thomas Sonnet #7

Trust heat of a noon-sun in its youth
Uplifted o'er heights attained in vigor
The rainbows give us the rain's truth
The arrows of living empty our quiver

Let winter steel us overjoyed by spring
Summer employs us autumn's succor
We take everything nature can bring
In time when our time's a sweet liquor

In bits our energy wears out by its use
We learn all we can in earth's school
What we are given no angels refuse
We take in and remember each rule

We give back as our thanks at each-turn
Our poems are our children that return

Shakespeare Sonnet #8

Music to hear, why hear'st thou music sadly?
Sweets with sweets war not, joy delights in joy:
Why lov'st thou that which thou receiv'st not gladly,
Or else receiv'st with pleasure thine annoy?

If the true concord of well-tuned sounds,
By unions married, do offend thine ear,
They do but sweetly chide thee, who confounds
In singleness the parts that thou shouldst bear.

Mark how one string, sweet husband to another,
Strikes each in each by mutual ordering;
Resembling sire and child and happy mother,
Who, all in one, one pleasing note do sing:

Whose speechless song being many, seeming one,
Sings this to thee: 'Thou single wilt prove none. '

Michael Thomas Sonnet #8

Not the words of husband, wife in anger,
discorded symphony it is a smash -
spaghetti on the wall the dish a banger
as women love less the men so rash.

The children keep the memory forever
screaming, in the closets of their mind.
Acquiring the guilt of others distemper,
this life can be so dark and so unkind.

We blame ancestors or society,
this-or-that condition of the soul,
temperature of blood propriety,
wistful excuses or mistaken goal.

Truth be told patience is more wise.
Wisdom gained from life a purer prize.

Shakespeare Sonnet #9

Is it for fear to wet a widow's eye,
That thou consum'st thy self in single life?
Ah! if thou issueless shalt hap to die,
The world will wail thee like a makeless wife;

The world will be thy widow and still weep
That thou no form of thee hast left behind,
When every private widow well may keep
By children's eyes, her husband's shape in mind:

Look what an unthrift in the world doth spend
Shifts but his place, for still the world enjoys it;
But beauty's waste hath in the world an end,
And kept unused the user so destroys it.

No love toward others in that bosom sits
That on himself such murd'rous shame commits.

Michael Thomas Sonnet #9

The widow winked out of door-less eyes
She leaned uprooted on a broken branch
Walking like a smoke trail toward skies
That extended their arms out by chance

Oh how we wish we could all get old nice
As a car disappearing down a lonely road
Where the memory of our wheels slice
The air into burnt out heaviness so cold

We open hearts to dangerous sympathy
Because it is easy to forget ourselves
In a falsity we will never get that way
But legs shake, hands number twelve

In the blurriness of our grey cataracts
We have no reference to ever go back

Shakespeare Sonnet #10

For shame deny that thou bear'st love to any,
Who for thy self art so unprovident.
Grant, if thou wilt, thou art beloved of many,
But that thou none lov'st is most evident:

For thou art so possessed with murderous hate,
That 'gainst thy self thou stick'st not to conspire,
Seeking that beauteous roof to ruinate
Which to repair should be thy chief desire.

O! change thy thought, that I may change my mind:
Shall hate be fairer lodged than gentle love?
Be, as thy presence is, gracious and kind,
Or to thyself at least kind-hearted prove:

Make thee another self for love of me,
That beauty still may live in thine or thee.

Michael Thomas Sonnet #10

The heart of hate in Paul that is germane
greed accrued to none to be dispersed.
Scrunch of face exceeded look of pain.
Snide of eye, lips tight and pursed.

Outlook dark when day is yet to die,
making charity the need to keep
heart hidden reasoning of why
stay awake count coins to sleep.

Maybe dad deserting made him so
or poverty his mother so complained.
To be near him made the light to go
leaving him left us feeling drained.

Love returns a kinder currency.
Misers earn worthless security.

Shakespeare Sonnet #11

As fast as thou shalt wane, so fast thou grow'st
In one of thine, from that which thou departest;
And that fresh blood which youngly thou bestow'st,
Thou mayst call thine when thou from
youth convertest.

Herein lives wisdom, beauty, and increase;
Without this folly, age, and cold decay:
If all were minded so, the times should cease
And threescore year would make the world away.

Let those whom nature hath not made for store,
Harsh, featureless, and rude, barrenly perish:
Look whom she best endowed, she gave the more;
Which bounteous gift thou shouldst in bounty cherish:

She carved thee for her seal, and meant thereby,
Thou shouldst print more, not let that copy die.

Michael Thomas Sonnet #11

We are more than life and death one-time-gone.
No god would endure a waste of all we gained.
Neither are we king nor queen nor lowly pawn
For our strength lies in remembering our pain.

Take the willow spread out in magnificence
Beneath its fan-tail swish is an earth it grew.
Dark musk earth sledged in worm opulence
Contains a history of a creation it once knew.

Always, we have nature to balance our fears:
Finite endings or infinite glorious continuance.
We sleep far from grace on an earth that steers
Between darkness and night starlight brilliance.

We speak of giving ourselves to a new future
In theory and fact we are permanent for sure.

Shakespeare Sonnet #12

When I do count the clock that tells the time,
And see the brave day sunk in hideous night;
When I behold the violet past prime,
And sable curls, all silvered o'er with white;

When lofty trees I see barren of leaves,
Which erst from heat did canopy the herd,
And summer's green all girded up in sheaves,
Borne on the bier with white and bristly beard,

Then of thy beauty do I question make,
That thou among the wastes of time must go,
Since sweets and beauties do themselves forsake
And die as fast as they see others grow;

And nothing 'gainst Time's scythe can make defense
Save breed, to brave him when he takes thee hence.

Michael Thomas Sonnet #12

Turned ribbons flown alight by winds
Passing day and circling the night.
Each built into a history that binds
Edges venturing around our fright.

Cruelty unkindness seems the core
Nature to dissolve itself in waste.
Of beauty come but leaving more
Bitter sweet as sour to the taste.

But thy kiss the lace of simple touch
Upon a memory of your sweet face.
Be you dead or alive there is much
Permanence that time cannot erase.

Sparrow you, wistful flowered grace
This a prayer my heart cannot replace.

Shakespeare Sonnet #13

O, that you were yourself! but, love, you are
No longer yours than you yourself here live:
Against this coming end you should prepare,
And your sweet semblance to some other give.
So should that beauty which you hold in lease
Find no determination: then you were
Yourself again after yourself's decease,
When your sweet issue your sweet form should bear.
Who lets so fair a house fall to decay,
Which husbandry in honour might uphold
Against the stormy gusts of winter's day
And barren rage of death's eternal cold?
O, none but unthrifts: -- Dear my love, you know
You had a father; let your son say so.

Michael Thomas Sonnet #13

You are who you are let no one say
you left a stone unturned a door closed.
Let the ledger balance up and pay
what's owed honest or what's proposed.

Deeds you bequeathed the world last
longer than the breath that you exhale.
Time stands still presently. The past,
returns to face us through the pale.

Actions we initiate come back,
in books, ideas, poetry and arts.
These are our children who attack
philosophies turned to new parts.

Everything discarded rises up to face
Higher spirits within our human race.

Shakespeare Sonnet #14

Not from the stars do I my judgment pluck;
And yet methinks I have astronomy,
But not to tell of good or evil luck,
Of plagues, of dearth, or seasons' quality;

Nor can I fortune to brief minutes tell,
Pointing to each his thunder, rain and wind,
Or say with princes if it shall go well,
By oft predict that I in heaven find:

But from thine eyes my knowledge I derive,
And, constant stars, in them I read such art
As truth and beatury shall together thrive,
If from thyself to store thou wouldst convert;

Or else of thee this I prognosticate:
Thy end is truth's and beauty's doom and date.

Michael Thomas Sonnet #14

Babylonian astrology;
Who, why, what, when where;
Encircling itself around history,
The wise providence we share.

The fool will die with never a clue;
Peasantry of common ignorance,
Clings to ego as if they never knew
Nature leaves not a thing to chance.

Before we're born we chose what we will be.
Assent of family tree, plots and tombs,
Conditions of our trials upon our entry,
Presage deliverance through our wombs.

We are more or less to always bide
Lifes we take and leave full of pride.

Shakespeare Sonnet #15

When I consider every thing that grows
Holds in perfection but a little moment,
That this huge stage presenteth nought but shows
Whereon the stars in secret influence comment;

When I perceive that men as plants increase,
Cheered and checked even by the self-same sky,
Vaunt in their youthful sap, at height decrease,
And wear their brave state out of memory;

Then the conceit of this inconstant stay
Sets you most rich in youth before my sight,
Where wasteful Time debateth with decay
To change your day of youth to sullied night,

And all in war with Time for love of you,
As he takes from you, I engraft you new.

Michael Thomas Sonnet #15

Heaven holds within its sacred vault
as natures sparkles then declines anon.
Thus we contain formulas, with no fault
displaying beauty once - forever gone.

If we look twice then never see an earth
as it was paradise twix sorrows.
Good and bad takes then returns a birth
restarting a new day from all tomorrows.

We can only live a life as flowers.
Our deeds will bring us back anon.
Deserts started out in spring showers.
We are adults of future companions.

Look to horizons for shadows of trees
Walking toward us on devout knees.

Shakespeare Sonnet #16

But wherefore do not you a mightier way
Make war upon this bloody tyrant, Time?
And fortify your self in your decay
With means more blessed than my barren rhyme?
Now stand you on the top of happy hours,
And many maiden gardens, yet unset,
With virtuous wish would bear you living flowers,
Much liker than your painted counterfeit:
So should the lines of life that life repair,
Which this, Time's pencil, or my pupil pen,
Neither in inward worth nor outward fair,
Can make you live your self in eyes of men.
  To give away yourself, keeps yourself still,
  And you must live, drawn by your own sweet skill.

Michael Thomas Sonnet #16

Chaos lies beneath thin layers of peace
waiting for any excuse to rue the day
when lover's love can no longer increase
and soft poetry turns to turgid melee.

Caution throws itself into fires of hate.
Ignorance holds sway over rational.
All history hides in ways that relate
to mayhem and hurt brought to hell.

I can tell you this: To thine own self
be secure against incoherency.
For, in quiet hours, in mind's shelf,
we face ourselves alone to eternity.

Cry not when thy freedom is want,
always "we are free" is heart's cant.

Shakespeare Sonnet #17

Who will believe my verse in time to come,
If it were filled with your most high deserts?
Though yet heaven knows it is but as a tomb
Which hides your life, and shows not half your parts.

If I could write the beauty of your eyes,
And in fresh numbers number all your graces,
The age to come would say 'This poet lies;
Such heavenly touches ne'er touched earthly faces. '

So should my papers, yellowed with their age,
Be scorned, like old men of less truth than tongue,
And your true rights be termed a poet's rage
And stretched metre of an antique song:

But were some child of yours alive that time,
You should live twice, in it, and in my rhyme.

Michael Thomas Sonnet #17

I do not have much faith in your daughter
For she is close minded, juvenile and sad.
Your son is a weak Hephaestus smith-er
And most all your family are basically bad.

If my love for you were put into words,
those words would fail to reach true merit.
For you are as genteel as angels heard
above the din of ordinary, you are fairest.

Nothing I could do to save my written tribute
of how you exemplify grace and sweet charm.
For etched stone dulls and books fade

Shakespeare Sonnet #18

Shall I compare thee to a summer's day?
Thou art more lovely and more temperate:
Rough winds do shake the darling buds of May,
And summer's lease hath all too short a date:

Sometime too hot the eye of heaven shines,
And often is his gold complexion dimmed,
And every fair from fair sometime declines,
By chance, or nature's changing course untrimmed:

But thy eternal summer shall not fade,
Nor lose possession of that fair thou ow'st,
Nor shall death brag thou wander'st in his shade,
When in eternal lines to time thou grow'st,

So long as men can breathe, or eyes can see,
So long lives this, and this gives life to thee.

Michael Thomas Sonnet #18

Nature's bounty fulfills itself by trade
In thy commerce with wealth of winds.
Green forests frequent thine eyes in jade.
Hush of your introspection wisdom lends.

Thy words upend oceans secret caves
Where flagellum dance, currents sway.
Dark night silent spirit veils wave
About thy sensuous lips, a passion play.

Oh! How you turn seasons into music song
A hot summer tango, you're falls serenade.
The winter of your patience lasts so long
And in thy fulsome ways spring is made.

Before your time there were no flowers save
But for thy smile each season's grace gave.

Shakespeare Sonnet #116

Let me not to the marriage of true minds
Admit impediments. Love is not love
Which alters when it alteration finds,
Or bends with the remover to remove:

O no! it is an ever-fixed mark
That looks on tempests and is never shaken;
It is the star to every wandering bark,
Whose worth's unknown, although his height be taken.

Love's not Time's fool, though rosy lips and cheeks
Within his bending sickle's compass come:
Love alters not with his brief hours and weeks,
But bears it out even to the edge of doom.

If this be error and upon me proved,
I never writ, nor no man ever loved.

Michael Thomas Sonnet #116

Cover thyself not in simplicity for love is more complex.
Answers that beg nae for understanding are nae the rule.
We give to others what others receive but do not index.
The gift that is remembered most is a love that is true.

In truth we carry no expectations of lies to be returned.
We cannot speak in error, that's spoken from the heart.
Ashes of endurance come only from passions burned.
Love's not shortened by time abjured as seasons start.

It is my eyes I give you to see my hands outstretched
embracing that softness of your breast's sweet bliss.
The breaths that die within your sighs are ascended
within the timeless airs above where all angels kiss.

Fret not of crept madness nor decay's insistence's.
Beside the winds of eternity is where our love rests.

Michael Thomas Sonnet #116-B

Tell all your friends who be married or divorced
To heed love, though seen thru anger or thru joy,
Was naught a penance but yea the proper course,
For fake or true it bestirs innocence a ploy.

And we who wish, whisper prayers of hope
Upon the altars of our broken dreams,
Or feel no love here at the end of a rope,
Awake! less passion deny love's esteems.

For as our lusts savored appetites,
Turning of the screw finds us adrift,
In hell to burn for Adam's apple bites.
With love our eyes open, hearts uplift.

Never was love's promise less or more,
A paradise to love the one that we adore.

Section Four –

Dante Divine Comedy

Mirrored (incomplete)

As Michael's Divine Comedy

Darkness: *Canto I The creature*, the speaker
and three followers of the written word. . . . . .

Torn from boyishness delusions so rife.
Adrift upon the meticulous considerations
of age and purchased elevated wisdom.

How so the path narrowed to perdition
or brightened into open directions clear,
my heart contained by fear but open eyed.

There upon the placements of sacred texts
sat the incoherent beast of disquiet-ness
with taut haunches and bespoken sulkiness.

"Please. " I said, "Is not courteousness thy way?"
(Hoping for a reaffirmation of accepted routine)
"Nae", did he say with a surly besmirched smile.

"Whence does the effort of kindness give a return?
Are you, as the rabble of ruin, a poet of ignorance?
Well, most would answer no, You stand amazed.

While most would believe their lies and covers,
your answers vary not nor alter this pointedness.
Differences erase the lines of similarities to heart. "

Terror of anger stifled my lack of affection for this creature as he shouted and ranted as one carried away by devils denying all interpretations that might mitigate his evil.

Thus the misguided poet spoke in wasted words until
to both of our amazement, songs of mirth and joy
came to our ears from three intrepid merry-men.
What surprise, was the three most renowned of all
who could place themselves in all history journals
and have their exploits upon the lips of all historians.

Homer: "Better to light a candle than to ... "
Virgil: ". . curse the darkness. Chinese proverb. "
Dante: "Turn up thy cups, friends of the light.

For we shall bless each other for the beauty,
for the heights of poetry yet to be surpassed,
yet to be enshrined within chronicles of ages. "

Homer: "Forebear, friends, who approaches?"
Aye, tis but the pseudo master of lays, Michael.
Ho, friend. Hello and why stalled with such fear?"

Dear, dear musicians of melodies. How wonderful
to find ye thus, in arm-in-arm and singing lustily.
It is the impediment of that creature we see

blocking the path and being a boor of bad bard
who curses all and misfits himself into spreads
of words like cannon shot that miss their mark.

Homer: "Are we not speakers of old? Be we
the carriers of deeds and misdeeds of those
not lettered in such afterthought or minds?"

Virgil: "Nae, not carriers but creators of that
for which history will point to as a truth. For
even squalid writings of ancients do but lie. "

Dante: "Oh, you two disparate angels of art,
Homer of truth and Virgil of fictions, neither
of you shall hold sway for reality is a mute blend. "

Michael: "Speak on but end this qualm for the
beast of anti beauty stands fixed in obdurate
rock-way to the path we all seek to pass through. "

When to our surprise a sacred angel of guidance
stood before us and with a placid smile said:
"To pass free, you must simply ignore the beast. "

And, disappearing from our eyes, also did the
creature of misspoken words so disappear
upon the broken horizon of scant luminescence.

Thus we four begin the path to where? We did
have no idea, but only our faith as writers and
observers of the frailty of indifferent humanity.

(continue)

Darkness: *Canto II. The descent.* Speakers protest
And the meeting of minds in birth and memory. . . . . .
. . . . .

Day found the arousal of leaf upon branch and restless stirrings of winged and wingless creatures reinventing themselves within the expanding light of their cautions.

To speak of us four, me, Homer in melodic speech, Virgil in musings and Dante as an exiled wanderer far from home, we were woken by the graces of a new unwritten day.

Please, sacred angels of the light,
compose me with space
of intentions clear and wary,
for to relate what I know and
do not know of tomorrow,
I shall relate in truth today.

For to speak of myself as human,

not so, but built upon the spirit and the divine pleasures of the flesh, so deign I to speak and pass through my manhood to be elevated.
Spoke I thus to the three parties of interest:
"Are we not beings of our beginnings? Or, are we but fragments of suspended egos held aloft with reconciling differences?"

Homer: "We are but adventures in emotion weighing what advantage we can gather by excellence and by the determinations of our sacred histories. "

Virgil: "But for love spilled upon the pages of responsibility, we are above the issues of regrets. Today we are but creators of myth. "

Dante: "To the weighing of guilt beside the

thin lines of forgiveness, we are but pilgrims upon a difference of prejudices . "

Yes, such truths be-spoken with grandeur.
Yet how such are these words spoken from the new mouths of untrained newborn babies?

If we listen to language, it is clear that concepts cannot be learned at such an early age when the softness of sleep is, to a baby, complete.

Thus, can we not infer that these souls, as we are, come from a place of knowing before the growing of life sets its pace?

Homer: "What's the variances of song when the time tells us, it is right to sing and life becomes life when day leads on. "
Ah, but cannot the beauty of your speaking, thus turned into tomes of such strength of Ilium turned ash by the hands of heroes,

leaving and landing on the waves of the
Aegean, Ionian and Mediterranean
shores of transparent grief and joy?

Are you but minor in significance?
Nae, whoso can add or subtract
from your great writing, man of words?

Virgil: "Neither man nor beast nor women
birthed in memory of such depth of
understanding can match your Homeric. "

Homer: "Softly. One such as your Aeneas
who filled the blanks of many minds with
intrepid mystery and myth of wonders. "

But, such as love and hate is not earned
by writing or growing old on the tree of
age. No, it is come inside our hearts

When the hearts came inside the
breasts of the wise and prudent
members of such animus wisdom.

Look! To the horizon is a visage
of one we know will come to
replace our wise words.

It is our father Chomsky who
attaches himself to Jungian
beliefs of pre-knowledge.

Hark, dear philosopher of
new days yet arrived. Do
you bring us what good life?

Chomsky: "Thus you all know
better than me, that our souls

are like the oceans around Greece.
Our souls are like the stars inset
to the silence of space as seen
from light years long since dead.

We come from yearnings of places
where our choices become our realities
manifest upon the womb of earth. "

Dante: " Are we become what we have
foisted upon us in experience from the
cradle to the causes of our deaths?"

Chomsky: "To the future Freudian and Skinnerian,
yes, it is only from that cause of environmental
accidents that we become what we are.

But, for the deeper thinking reasons, we
were alive in spirit before we were alive,
and all time is spacious without divisions. "

Let us proceed down this vacant path of
discussions. And, are you to stay with us
on our journey, dear language master?

Chomsky: "It is with sadness that I watch
you four recede into the levels of horizons
and into the expanses of places I cannot go.

Forever, I will read and understand all your
lovely words and ideas, but only from the
pages of the written memorials of your lays. "
And then he disappeared and we four became
as the wind moving without motion over a
graceless path from whence we knew not.

(continue)

Darkness: *Canto III.* The continuing of downward path into the realms of greater darkness and mists where-onto the poet cries for lost love that leads to clarity in understanding. . . . .
. . . .

Whence the bitter night not dissolved by day
lay over the approaching storm of dissident
evil and hate, we moved by small degree forward,

that metre and motion could but be measured
only in compact receptacles of finite blocks
of an infinite nature between our increasing doubts.

Toward the direction-less approach we knew not
a point of fixture, but only faint hope that we were
in line with some obscure magnet to bleak parts.

As we wound with our eyes fixed to the footfall
of fear, in the distance arose a lady (my lady)
of whom so many of my hearts had invested

a time and chance of endeavor that consumed
all too many years of servitude to her bidding
regal composure of demanding compliance's.

Spoke I thus to her with many cautious fervors
within my remaining hope of redemption:

Michael: "For you the sun was cascaded within the times when only your visage was my landscape.
For you, my eagerness to be humbled by
your vicissitudes lay open my soul to ridicule.

Oh, such smallness of ego was my greatest
gift to you, Persephone, and now why do you
block the way to where I must sever your ties?"

Persephone: "Tell me, little soul, what have you gained by withdrawing yourself these last years? Have you earned the inner respect you lacked in my presence?"

Homer, Virgil and Dante: "Talk not to him as such. "

Michael: "Please, to be divided by love is to be whole in life.
Truth - that fixtures became fallacies of meanings.

I have lasted out the pain of perseverance and
kept within myself all the times of your angers
which fell upon our feelings like a false shield. "

Persephone: "You needed me to laugh at yourself. "

Michael: "Yes and to learn the strength of diligence in duty. I have separated the placements of our days

And never can you call absurd the beauty of the hawk
that we captured in silence between the arched wood
and walk way of undisputed nature where even the

birds became winged angels of adventure among
the branch and shadows of leaning tree trellis.
To become the green growth in our eyes as

banded fern binding the muscled tree rooted earth
in patches of curved entrees delicious pallets
of delicacies sized to wishes of the emerald leaf.

We were one in amazement at the secrets of

mushrooms collected in pods of pleasures
bedecked by moss and broken branch cover."

Persephone: "You speak so eloquent of romance.
But nature is mean and decisive in its duties. "

Michael: Oh, sweet lover of my days, how mean,
but in ways of Shiva to bring new beauty from
within its bowels and bowers of filaments.
For Vishnu sustains what Brahma builds. "

Persephone: "Have you forgotten our Lord Jesus?"

Michael: No! Never forgotten only replaced by a higher understanding where redemption is kept within my reaches and not upon a cross of sorrow.
Gather what you have, my sweet lady, of
our gardens placed so calculated with beauty.
Take the sweet lilies in July forever. Keep the
moist bell-flowers and burnt iris shyness blue.
Form your heart of the colors we grew together.

Fill your heaven with the heartiness of our work
upon the fences and patches of a god's creation,
that we had on loan in spaces of petals and plants. "

Persephone: "So where does that leave us now student?"

Michael: "No longer your schooling of neediness in trade for this nobility of spirit, I divest myself of your tenders.

I am inviolate in love with what truths are propounded
by our association of decades of festive and favored
happiness when we were new to each other in lace

and litanies of magical ceremonies. Now, begone to

your immense needs of instruction, away from me.
Be who you are as Persephone without Michael in tow.

Be away from us, for we four proceed to a fate
not determined but of which we are not in fear
only in warnings of what exists inside our tortured

meanings and intelligences. Go, my sweetest of
womanly graces. Go to distances where you
fade in my heaviness of meanings and parts. "

(continue)

Darkness: *Canto IV.* The tortured path and the
discussion of mysterious things of danger that
treat fear as wishes...

Homer: "Masters of words. We find ourselves
caught by eternity. Can this path be a symbol
for hell or a cause for redemption from it?"

To place a wafer of communion upon our tongues
does not transfer the loaf of bread into our bellies.
We are neither hell-bent nor heaven-sent in longevity.

Homer: "To what purpose do we need a hell? Is
the desire for damnation an ace card we hold for
our enemies? Neither are we desirous of heaven.

When the doors of eternity swing both ways, that
will be the end to hell and paradise. But we are not

interested in a cause for our egos, we want
affirmation. There was a soul that passed to their
heaven. The guides created as much of that soul's

desires, as possible. When the limits had been reached, the soul begged for a death to begin again the cycles of love that it missed so much within its heart.

Homer: "Why were these loves not within its paradise?"

Because love needs a platform of hate to mirror itself upon. Paradise cannot contain anything but love, and therefore the distinction becomes blurred,

as almost nonexistent. To have an earth of flowers we need an earth mixed with volcanoes as well we know - one lends itself to the other.

Virgil: "This journey, like my Aeneas following his path, is one of differences. Did my Dido die for love or hate?She did die of loneliness for her lover sailing off to Rome. "

Dante: "There is your reason for hell - loneliness is a hell all by itself. There seems to be no end to reason when we are lonely. I, deserted by my peers, know it."

Homer: "Your hell, Dante, is your choice. You could have conformed and stayed with the ones you loved. You chose your own hell and now all you have is to write of it. "

Dante: "But, choosing the correct political path, could have been a worse hell than banishment. " Homer: "To choose one hell for another is a god's predicament. "

You three become immersed within Pythagorean syllogistic thinking. Dante: "Well maybe hell is only numbers that do not resolve themselves in extremes even worse than pi. " We have made no headway toward the path to darkness.

Virgil: "Where is this path to take us? We are as slaves to some dark territory of the mind. " Homer: "Yes, yes. "

There, upon the center of the path is the obstacle to our continuance - the dark center of unknowing. That is the one hindrance to our proceeding into the black night.

The fear of it is greater than the darkness itself. We have a construct in Emmanuel Kant - The darkness is replicated to the point of the symbol it represents in a mirrored strata.

Homer: "Tis a bit confusing to me. I prefer a battle where the darkness is the death of a hero who leaves a legacy of tears and bravery for his deeds upon helping others.

It is honorable to fear. I once feared the limits of obscurity and it led me to write and transfer this fear to my heroes. "

Virgil: "Well done my great friend of tragedy. Well done. "

(continue)

Darkness: *Canto V*. The path, the desert, the cries of the baleful begging forgiveness and passage out of the halo of stagnant miseries. . . . .
. . . .

Through the blinding fog of pitch distances collected into compressed ions of ebony canvas flat breathless as the exhale of equatorial drafts removing all moisture, from the latitudes of deserted stretches of dryness cold to the nostrils and hot to the mid sun burning of sand and small insects that acclimate to the oven of unbearable vice gripping manacles of dune prisms, where the cries of faithless voices came to our ears. Could it be the locked-in evaporation of our lost days?

Here on the lapped junctures of waterless valleys
and hillocks of striated wind-blown ribbons of arid
voided blankets showing wrinkles in row-upon-row.

Here is where the mind cannot conceive of endless
but picture of plenitude-inside-plenitude ad nauseous

relentless repetition of eager insanities of ingratitude.

Colors of faint swirls rising out of the whispering
pockets of compressed particles like waking dust
bins of brindled silent storms inside the gold haze.

Atop the clamor of bronze wishes in ever growing
suspensions of voices that quietly scream for release
alone in their complaint but together in their chorus.

Crying as if wounded creatures proclaiming an
innocence of guilt while holding in their sound all
the indications of their sordid intransigence.

We four held fascinated by this ocean of dirt that
had become a shifting movement of surfaces
speaking out in cankerous cacophony of ill designs.

Never in bottomless wells forgotten impatient
emptiness with dangled buckets sash saying
on frayed ropes of hopeless banging along

the descending earthen tunnels conical drops
of echoing sadness, were the hanging souls
of soulless penitents screeching their sins into

the battered wailing darkness. We cringed in
empathy for these scraping sentiments of
black sacraments of sorrow-over-sorrow.

Homer: "Agamemnon's ships bestirred by
angry seas could not have been written as
this vast quickness of burnt ash imaginings.

Washed shores of Circes beaches would
have turned these wasted waves aside
and prayed for rain as singing psalms. "

We cannot go further, my friends.
There are limits to these human canticles
as no orchestra could reduce to kindness.

Virgil: "I can only return to the wailing
of sad death streams of Troy in its finality
of fires and tears beside the mask of Hector. "

We must forebear for patient waiting for a way
past the furnace and flames of this heaving
breathless torrent of cries and colored red bands.
Even the blessed angels have distanced themselves
from their comrades of faceless fallen forgotten ones
who dwell in non-existence of space of airless ways.

Dante: "The path you take is not clear, my master
Michael. And you have yet to see and feel what is

your fate as designed by forces beyond your control. "

To what venues do you propose, having been as one baptized and brought out from determinations of death?

Dante: "Only you can create your wishes. My day is done. "

But you accompany us as an aide to understanding, and we all look to you for explanations of these massive measured ways.

Dante: "Only your measures shall be your detriments and joys. "

But, tell me, dear friend. Is not nature redundant in these paths we retake as you once took them? Are we not a mirror of your reflective honors and medals of attainment?

Dante: "Each has their heaven. Each has their hell.
Only love and hate recur in measured vessels of spirit.
To want my way, would only lead to you not discovering.

Your enchantments are not my nightmares.
Your blandishments are my splendors replete
with affections and delicate salvation of grace.

To be what you are is to be singular in fashions
and familiar ways that only you can remember
within your over-soul umbrella of haven life's"
This terrible place misuses my brain with fervid
detachments, and on we must go or else
perish within the vacuum of this temperament.

I cry to you my Lord to bring us forth from here,
as my companions are at a loss for leverage and
motion of escape from this cauldron of chaos.

Beside the ambush of arrogance arose a white
feathered bird so large that none of the horizon
could hide from its wings outstretched invitingly.

There are mysteries, even in the ways of darkness,
where elements of cause become inverted to being
elements of affectation that suspend blessings thus.

To our wonderment, all four of us were swooped

within the span of this aviary savior, and pulled into
the squalid hot air, swept past the camphor billows,

brought up past the curling cylinders of fast furious
baked fingers of the desert in confessional firmament,
alighted upon cooler softer clouds of movements.

And there we sallied as on a caliph's carpet of lightness over the terrific fanned lifeless singed earth below from up we went across to a place none of us comprehended.

(continue)

Darkness: *Canto VI*. The reading of scrolls placed as puzzles to madness and despondency. . . . .

Text: Fear not thy innermost dilemmas of faith

for I shall sever your mind from all gods

of safe harbor and banish you to bounds

that confine each part of redemption into
closed compartments of unremitting despair.
Trust only tomorrow to corpses of stillness.

Relive the advent of wickedness and become
as equal to the binges of breaking lies forced
open to eyes of skeletal remains in anguish.

To all who read, close thine eyes for understanding.
Open thy ears to only the pitch sleep of deep silences
and touch all favors with the union of black fingers

as leprosy unclothed to the wasting cloth of winds
in sync with musty memories of pain and dishonor.
You are entered into contests of death as claimants.

Michael: "These words go on in nefarious ways
and I keep open the pages of recall with bitterness
as in an envelope of sentiments of sacred nothings. "

Text: Come you with open hearts of burdened blessings like as coal within a chalice of dried blood and dust. Come you with a prayer for reversal of salvation's.

Michael: "These words get as worse than blank
terror of my misunderstandings gone wild to weep.
Tear open this tale and canvas the stars that care."

Text: Bundled as twigs for weak wood to lament
Take not heart in wasted winters dissolved
upon the thaw of miscreant bones disarrayed.

Homer: "Can the mind compete with these texts?
Neither is there word left to secrete any honey from

these discolored thoughts that make my writing die."

Virgil: "Dear friend. We are secure for a time that is delayed by the dearth of these tellings come as dark from the bowels of an hole of understandings. "

Text:
Honor is a pale price to pay for advantage.
Keep thy pride as the earth swallows all
of your eyes with quick drinking in shells.
Where the bird sang, now the wind cries.
Where the morning woke, now darkness.
And, where the darkness had eyes blind.

Upon the footfalls of warriors blood dries
as a cankerous stain of cameo guild bled
brown, a bake of a musk parched earth.

Tender as the telling of transference from
one heart to a black hole of luster-less days.
I am the coming apart of all written links.

Michael: "We have been placed upon this bleak place to discover your words contained in jars of lost memories long before Shin-eqi-unninni.

Long before Enheduanna extolled queen Inanna.
Is not Grendel to be redeemed rather than lost?
And "flowery" sirens drowned within their songs."

Dante: "Our task is clear. We must overcome these texts of such dire foretelling. We must to a new path emerge and deliver our message true."

Michael: "It is clear that from the beginning of life "word" was cast upon the collected meanderings of ape or human endeavor suspended into time.

To say: "In the beginning was the word and
the word was with god and god was the word"
is concurrent with language in all forms.

The god is incidental to the word, since the word
surpasses the god in significance borne upon the
pages of all languages and cultures of differences."

Text: Tempt me not with language of mercenaries
for I am the word that erases all other sounds
and my breath shall dissolve the Babel towers

as well as all edifices of words built upon themselves
even in pyramids and skyscrapers or cities spread
within the oxygenated gravities of spacial orbits.

I am the chosen one and the messiah and the sword
of Islam come to cut open the beast of words in
battle and peaceful enclosures with immeasurable pity.

Close not your books to my place of encroachments.
Cover not your faces from the blinds of my solar-ness.
Even as the stars become dull, I shall shine forever.

Michael: "We must turn to all the peace within our hearts to avoid the ballast of beastly words that sear at our minds. We must learn new Greek tongues that dissolve into Latin.

We must incorporate the street jargons into the dictionaries

of our souls where inch-by-inch our salvation is won in word and our heaviness of spirit is lightened by the grace of tongue. "

Text: O saving victim, opening wide

the gate of heaven to all us below
For whence I come to close the gate
and place the bricks upon Jerusalem forever

Then, to the enclosure of space and tablets
arranged in order of mayhem as flown
above the earth in elevations of words

angels of lightness and grace spread a
blanket of understanding beneath the
texts of ancient murmurings to uplift

and to further the path for the travelers
of written word to proceed upon their task
to bring new life to the minds of written hearts.

(continue)

Darkness: *Canto VII*. The dolorous opening
of new sadness to befall the travelers of truth. . . . . .

We came to a wood enclosed with soundless
meditations of nature as the crickets and bird
scratching's upon branch and broken ground.

Here all creatures busied themselves quietly
seeking food in caches of plunder over small
insects or berries buried beneath the bower.

A wending bank bespoken stream rippled over
the silences in mesmerizing patterns of water
gurgling in repeating convergent sequences.

Homer: "We sorely need to collect our thoughts.
So swift the passage of tense advancements must
be calmed to release the pressure of such visages. "

Virgil: "To allay our fears, this glen of natural clime
seems just tonic to the traveler seeking justice as
we do with much constraint upon our criticisms. "

Dante: "Yes, it is so to us who ply the dangerous
elements so as to complete our understandings,
though adding much, much grimace to our souls.

But, what! My master Michael, do we but see
a quiet denizen of this bucolic evergreen home?
Is it not a man bent forward, sitting without eyes

as a wounded pilgrim upon the layered bank near
the resounding stream of hypnotic consequence?
Yes it is he we know not but must address, Ho!,

Ho! Fine sir. We are but passing between points
unknown to us only in adventures of mysteries.
And do you also travel, my fine seated friend?"

Michael: "He speaks not. I have sounded him

and with no words, he tells of the sadness of
calumny placed upon his being as a malediction.

To wit, a social blame of degrees of intransigence
spoken out and carrying the weight of disdain
by other unknowing souls of peers who sneer. "

Homer: "What! Here in this haven of placidity
there is a blast of bad behavior mocking this place?"
Michael: "Speak low, to the heart of this man. "

Chorus of Voices: Wither does the just complaint

and the advantage of miscalculation fall upon him
who tries to convert the crimes of others to cure.

We stand useless to the un-forgiven cancers that
eat away the gain of him who is branded unfairly.
Curses upon the intransigent soul is not our way.

But, patience and understanding set quietly inside
our hearts to bring about the desired effect of

example to this wet-eyed soul of imagined guilt.

Michael: "Is this but another sadness? To be in paradise yet to be in hell for souls to stand in shame for crimes they never imagined? Then open this door, please, that we may all see wherein others carry the same penance within. Open the great door that holds us back from deeper knowledge of such calamity. "

Chorus of Voices: Please, please do not open
the door that closes out the ministrations of
far too deep complexities of sorrows that lie

waiting to vex even the most collected minds
of fair and law seeking wise men in combines
partnered with others of their true natures.

Michael: "Our favored friend, Charles Dickens said:
"Tis but another example of child hating the parent,
or brother against brother, anon, repeating itself
over."

Chorus of Voices: You four shall never know
the eyes of missing sight and hearts of no kindness
that collect themselves in wailing pools of madness.

None shall see the families of discontent rending
their gatherings into baleful hurts and miseries.
No, it is not to us to open this door. None we know.

You four and all who will follow you, will pass without ever seeing the obverse panels of unremitting pain that lie on the inside of this door. Awake away.

Interlude of Simplicity

We cannot sing of heaven when we seek love for all our life is made of weary dreams that collide with the silk and strife of more than a velvet touch you bring me captions of blue corridors that soothe me as I fly into a deepest purple hue.

You are my fingers that fret for a day of precious spangles of whimsical wishes upon the once upon a time of fables guided by a beam of broken rainbow that fixes up the sky with eye to the colored banded layers of inky-winky-why

(continue)

Darkness: *Canto VIII*. A prayer interlude

We came upon a place of incense and mist
inside imagined walls of a cathedral mustiness
formed around the base of stars and moons.

Here tender faced men in mannequin stillness
sat cross-legged in obscured indifference of
supreme smiles and inward satisfactions.

Undisturbed by our presence as immobile fixed
within their daze and delivered distances of mind
adrift, alight as crinkled velvet prayers intoned -

Om Mani Padme Hum set as in-vocative psalm
of repeating sequences in linked consciousness
discoursed in musical variances and timbre.

We four were taken into the veil of changes
where our voices reacted to the communion
of selfless actions and companionship.

Before the golden sympathies escaping out
of the curlicues of sounds, there formed a
wondrous collective hymn as ambient air.

It hung itself in timelessness encased by
patchouli, musk, jasmine, sandalwood,
peppermint, vanilla - rich embodiments

of bubbled blends of fragrant essences
surreal all distributed within our beings -
intangible banquets of sachets of lace

extending their odoriferous inheritance
equally, impartial fan-like peacock tails,
succor-savored serenaded imploring

cautious, begging of supplications to
an invisible aura of oracle inquiry.
Beseeching all temperate gods.

Our sustained entreaty as powdered
deliverance's laid end-to-end
up-and-down
sideways
ubiquitous,

becoming a goading of grief and joy,
telling of tales of hidden happiness,
remembering all empathy of love.

This dispassionate donation to angels
as intermediaries between doorways
of symbolic treasure rooms of praying

became as entering or exiting the
mysterious libraries of light in
diffused delicacies.

Homer: "I cast my causes out of
the separate words of my being
and into the pot of prayerfulness. "

Virgil: "It is as my enervated size
of sorrows that I lend a spaced
lightness to the mechanics of this.

I empty that part of me that only

knows truth and wishes of worlds
to be exposed as tributes of wise. "

Dante: "Upon the busy streets
of my distant Florence, I walk
in veiled secrecy to touch the

cloth of my family and feel the
loss of their joy in my absence,
as an expiation here in humility. "

Michael: "To the delicate days
of youth and ideology burned
into a brand upon my mind,

I give away those pleasures
of past and transfer my thoughts
to the emptiness of time-within-time. "

God: It is to my benefice that your words
are received into my special covenant.

I give back to all of you a peace of heart
to keep you safe as your journey goes on.

I place a net of my grace around you
and keep you with the markings of me.

Go, now, leave only a thought within
the offertory of my tabernacle.

Go to the places of my visions
and return to me the change
of all your transactions.

(continue)

Darkness: *Canto IX. The night speaks*

Whence narrowed confines of passage related to
our minds of safety becoming less as loneliness
and unworthy placements within our thoughts,

the night evolved into a slow wrenching of words
that tightened our throats and made our breath
in gasping coughs of foreign feelings of discomfort.

We four men of strength, each in each other's way,
watched each other's eyes express deeper fears
as mists formed into whispers that demeaned.

Here is the slow descent into a screech of vowels
strained nuances of literal meanings become as
wafer thin slices of sounds terrible in extremity.

Eerie wafting of sing-song blurred words that
made interpretation impossible. We four
dissolved into the demonic distributions
of a language of impossibilities. Homer:

"Heaven-less hangings onto a gorge
of gargantuan dizziness descending. . . . . . . "

Virgil: "descending descending descending. . . . . . "

Dante: "descending deep into a place so
dark as to impede movement as if the
cavernous night had glued us within it. "

Homer: "Yes, entombed as pith of
a corpse that is no longer recognizable. "

Dante: "Nor revitalized in any construct
of cohesiveness. A blend of unbound
beseeching syllables uttered in vain. "

Night Voices:
Give yourselves to infinity of your dying.

Robert Louis Stevenson: (Requiem)
Under the wide and starry sky

Dig the grave and let me lie:
Glad did I live and gladly die,
And I laid me down with a will.

This be the verse you grave for me
Here he lies where he longed to be
Home is the sailor, home from sea,
And the hunter home from the hill.

Night Voices: Rest in the arms of my grip
and voice For all is nothing. You forfeit choice.

Homer:
I am blind to see black
wall of many words
I cannot retract
what's said or heard

Virgil
I close my eyes
to close my lies
Please don't keep
Words I weep
Unfair mistakes
Never to wake

Gounod - Requiem
I am the sweetness of voices to temperate airs
alive with lucidity and discernment of melodies.

Death come to the movement of my baton
and let the cello and violin part the space
where my thoughts become a prayer for you.

Night Voices: Your death is not a melodic choral interlude. It is a wrenching of your lungs denied air.
It is a spasm of your extremities in vain.
Your death is a black mass of soulless sound.

Michael: Together in binds of silver lace
we shall weave a pliant of words
that comfort you in your longings for love.
We shall surrender ourselves for your heart
to rise above the line of fear and above the lift
of angles where oblique light will lead you to a path divine.

Night Voices:
Mistaken in all but their despondency,
these wanderers of wishes unredeemed
do traverse the punitive pathways of doom.

Colorless, vapid, enervated as a conch shell
free floating on the scud and swirl ocean floor
of demerits and dangers, these try our patience.

(continue)

Darkness: *Canto X. Oceanic Tears*

Whence our path dissolved into a sweeping
line of a thousand jagged edges of sandy
water tips as the seeming blinded horizon
of aqua stretches to a long level being
out of reach but so close to our perceptions.

A distance as a blind man could never complain of
so far away that even small birds were dissolved
within the vapors of this liquid chalice of bleach
blood seeped to the blue of wavelets incessant.

We four stood mute against the whistling waves
crashing as orchestras dying in moaning melodies.

We four stood transfixed by the crash of hillocks
of water rushing toward a land that drew the
dissolving back-rush of swirls into a miasma
of sand-sucking movements that seemed to
be as a blotter taking and giving back the
semblances of designs on the glittering beach.

A beach that was so dark it shone forth in ebony
silhouettes of shaded mists shaped by silver edges
intoning a splurge of final walls of water ending.

And as these concurrent plates of viscous measures
washed up and washed back to the pool of its eyes
of immeasurable vastness, there came a rising
catch of choruses spending themselves in choking

complaint of deep sadness as only an ocean can contain in its basins of burdens and blandishments.

A chorus of indistinct crying as litanies of regret, psalms of pain, songs of sorrows, pleadings and begging's for answers to such blurred questionings as insane unrecognizable phrasings and words.

A disconnected band of vibrations that collected themselves into a mayhem of incoherency.

We four attempted, by becoming fixed in attention, to discern the meanings and temperaments of

these dehumanized baleful wizened thin arching's.

Nothing made sense. All was confusion.
A fear of the gyro spinning into emptiness
overtook us as the circle of ocean mist
begin to form into panels of wordless tears.

"Who are you calling us from the edges of this depth and infinite swell of black inequality?" said Homer as he knelt with his head bowed.

Virgil: "Tell us not of your terror and tone of ingrown bewilderment. We are but human and cannot decipher the canticles of canker. "

Ocean Lament: We are the payment in full for the over demands of society racing toward an invisible misery of emptiness. We are the stains of variant discontent for destinies of waste and wanton wickedness sowed in greed.

We are the severed shipwrecked souls of ingratitude that passed over the child and parent of hungriness.

We are the ballast of waste and garbage left to rot
on the shores and shoals of a bandaged barrier reef
where the sponge dried in disease and the delicate
sea anemones wilted into black flakes of filaments.
Where the once brilliant coral spheres sank to death.
And the edges of nestled enchantment disappeared.

We are the wasted depths of what was once seed
of all creatures and landscapes that became what
we imagined them to be in the evaporated segues.

From the creeping of crustacean embodiments
of the crab and the isopods compacting their
skeletal impressions upon the silted parchments
of these overlapped remarkable historical events:

From the alluvial sea amphipods and Ostracods
and ignorant bedeviled sand fleas of pestering

insistence's that drove emerging species to die:

We are the whorls of emaciation. We are the
flaying filaments of dusty remnants of endless
possibilities that became and undid their days
in experimental obscuration of blurred energies.

Never become misled by our layers that continue
to phase and follow every possibility into envelopes
of insertions and exhaustions of seeming wastelands.
We are the singing stretches of sea caves hiding
the embodying differences of designs of the
shepherd and the flocks of school fisheries.

To our sad choruses of reliquaries that overstepped
their griefs with joyous emergence's of ghost shrimp
and salamanders leaving their trails of trials imprinted,

to the silliness of octopus evolving into alligators

to the snapping of turtles holding the victims of

their hungers underwater to die, we celebrate
the erosion of our surfaces as canvas to create.

Michael: "How can we begin to call forth meanings
out of this porridge of sentences that scathe our ears
and reduce us to impotent poets of pecuniary pence.

This descendant crumbling wall of alabaster musts
blocks our understandings and mars our visions.
We are waylaid and abandoned upon the combs
of crashing cries that shame us by their shrieks. "

Ocean Lament: You are the advantageous
fat bellied Buddha's. You praise yourselves
with effervescence of empty egos.

You are the decline of the meanings of text
that laid the mysteries before you and will
renew them without your poetry.

Proceed, proceed on your ridiculous journey

for the ends of all being will engulf you in their
hidden sources and replace what vapidness
needs replacing from the drained pages of
the books that you structured your life within.

Dante: "Do not mock us by your eminence.
Did we not so suffer to draw out the best
of all intentions by our memories stretched
to the fullest of their abilities? We made the
ultimate sacrifice of denying pleasure to sit
with pen and waste out our days writing so
that generations would come to new tales. "

Ocean Lament: Pish! Your new tales are
void of all reductions of foregone "speakers"

who carried the myths forward by only their
recitations from anxious ears to ears who
sat silent in hearing what life was before them.

Not one of you four self-praised announcers
could contain within your training the pinned

poetry that came out of their mouths as
living books of requiems and remembrances.

Give a congratulation to the wise ones
who brought up the level of consciousness
by sacrificing their days in memorization
and structured stories.

Go, now you are released to judge and jury
these things into brand new births of books
and we shall wait for your new Troys to
rise up from the joyful operas of Helen
and Paris leading Greek ships to new
sheltered shoals. We shall reawaken
Dido and let her stand naked to the
winds of weathered times. We shall
allow you to bring souls down to and
up from all the hells of your imaginings.

Darkness: *Canto XI. Choral Interlude*

Chorus I:
See the antipodal poets of estranged distances.
They write inside and out of their gifted essences.

Chorus II:
Would we have their powers, we would be set free
from our observations of day-to-day extremities.

Chorus III:

Sing thus with us brothers and sisters a song
of the despair of ages of days long gone by.
Sing and make us feel the words go deep.

Chorus of sorrows:
When the days of our deliverance
collided with the gainsay precious
jeweled alliances of speaking's,

from the gloves of our faces
tight to the waking sentences
of our hankering obsessions
came the songs of sounds
that mimicked the burdens
cast upon the tables lean
laid with all the wild feasts
that we partook in reverie.

Oh, easy was the doing
of things that had no thought
when we gave away what we had not bought
and played the fool for love in our absent minded naught

Oh, easy was the doing
of the touch and simple wooing
between the thorn and blush rose blooming
that we purchased with pleasures that became our undoing ection Four – Excerpt Of Dante Divine Comedy Mirrored (Incomplete)

Section Five –

Poems Of The Rabbi –

Patricia, Lewis And Me

Chapter One

Poems of the Rabbi
Buddha V
when we write we channel
to the ancients for clarity

spending overnights at
Homer's house
evacuating sing-song

playing rain-barrels
with Dido and Virgil

pleasures of Gilgamesh,
Enheduanna crawl over
spans of time, immeasurable

then calls the lessons of
Greece, Rome, metamorphosed
by Ovid or paraphrased by Marcus Aurelius:

"A man should be upright, not kept upright. "
"Be content to seem what you really are. "

say what we have to say
remember Dante's way

curl your toes around Milton's prose

become mesmerized by W. Shakespeare
bend to the modern Eliot, or Pound

it is not such a mystery:
either we learn the past
or keep patting our own backs

Life

Sang-froid of life is
surrender to death
with forbearance.

Death comes upon us
slowly as a life builds
its memories.

Finesse of obeisance,
sublime humility,
deference to mysteries,
earth put proper to rest.

When the breath becomes short
there is an air of
oboes playing
  for us
    in a star-way
      of love.

Michelangelo, Carvaggio, Edouard Manet
Delighted in art in a certain way
Their forms distinct and recognizable
They collect up on walls like bible

Dali
Pollock
Kandinsky

strip, take all your clothes off
lay them in a pile and stand back
each one of you, remove your arms
slip out of your head and bend

for those that are able, fall flat
and change into patches of ink melted
those remaining, please take your neighbors
arm, leg, attach them to your self anywhere

all of them squeeze onto an imperfect pin
some of them speak to spectacles
many of them hold a fate inside a bottle
lots of us try hard to penetrate rocks
all of us watch the others

one of us is dying faster than expected
two of us are being tested by him
he holds death in a clench of contest
two of them are my friends
friends I will never desert
amplitude confines my patience with two of them
professions of faith are forgotten by the one dying
dying consumes his every moment
she and I know that he is weak
his fear is surprising

I collect words in a cache of silence
I swear that my death will never be a war
faith is knowing that a God or an agent of God
  is always watching - waiting to help
all of us know something greater than us exists
all of us will be given love in the end

Music

Preludes Op. 28

Gingerly we step into the sphere
where words become obscured

re - sid - u - als
tran - scend - ing
com- ple - ments

chop chop chop chop Chopin

plunk plunk plunk plunk plunk plunk
come absinthe September boozy
col - lect - ions, re- flec- tions
af - fec - tions, pre - cep - tions

time delay plunk plunk plunk plunk
hurry, scurry, worry, blurry plunk plunk

invascular impertentions ovacated
joy-sensuous cavities
plunk plunk plunk plunk plunk plunk

cafasciposien swelter of leaf spangled

toward newer hearts opened air of tender
love fingered to tune of evaporating colors

that sweet breath of you
inside my ear
autumn liquor

In Fondling Youth Allays Time To Spare

In fondling youth allays time to spare
Nor flower fades nor aspiration flies
Into the link where continuity lies
Innocent where angels do not care

Slowly how the mind sweetly knows
Little clues awareness builds a nest
Excluding less, including but the best
In gardens weedless love but grows

Time erodes confidence season's lust
Turns cold winter minds to sleep anon
Buried beneath leaf-of-life all begone
In heaven's heart plied doubt-to-dust

There were burdens broken and bent
But sealed within our soul's testament

Fifty

At fifty I divided into two parts
one of time past and another empty.
I sewed my memories into one lining
of my long cotton faded blue robe.

Each morning I slipped new dreams
into the pocket of the empty side
until, now, at one hundred years
the garment falls evenly over toes.

With careful attention I restitched
the one side and sewed in the new.
Now, as I go about my days alert
to birds in trees and suns arising,

I carry an empty place in my heart
as a repository for breezy aromas
like the scandalous skunk at midnight
or the occasional cry of an infant

carried over the rooftops near me
informing me that all desire spent
leads to some new beginnings of life,
where autumn will continue to unfold.

Embarrassment

these numbered blinks
she counts as his love
various shades of lies

mom held a blanket
around us on the beach
after training / before pubes

there, before us, are the
insecure universes always awake

at least, we sleep, therefore
we are not solar mysteries

she pretends his constancy
is due to her allure
singular phenomenon

his advanced notions
comfort him that she

will always be there
to cover his changing
in and out of perfection

they both hide their shame
as those around them sneak-peek

Heat

I know the heat of summer
can erode desire.

Two forces collide
you sleep.

I watch the stars
pillowed in comfort.

The moon stretched
by clouds.

Simple resonance of
Lake Superior swaths
your sand cushioned thighs.

There is an indentation of you
above me, pressed into my heart -
where you collapsed earlier and
drowned in giggles.

Can we really believe that Winter
or beach crowds will stay away?

The darkness is complete and only
some strange fish secretly watch
as you drape innocence into silts
of backwash - clever little waves
of amber glint to the shadows over you.

I knew this had an ending.
It would have done no good to
beg time.

Every little tweak of your pleasure,
indistinguished from the suppressing
sweat of pores cascaded down a slope
of enjoyment mixed into receding water,
with no return.

Civil War

The belly full of hatred that spills out of us
when we see our friends cry for their mothers, dying.
The fear that turns our legs to absolute liquid
making us sit, unable to move or think, crying.

The splotches of red on walls, ground and trees
where life came to an abrupt final ending.
The dark night of flares and tracer rounds from
fifty calibers making us believers of blessings.

The emptiness of silence from a crazy moon ignoring
the screams and chaos of young souls confused.
Ten times I banged my helmet against the furrowed
foxhole to test whether or not I was imagining.

Then the sky opened and Caesar was talking with
Achilles as ships burned in the Hellespont.
The ground broke loose from Lincoln's tears at
Gettysburg as B-29s firebomb Tokyo.

The lost wail of civilians in all history of war
cried to me out of the black stars.
And never will I ever sleep as in a trance of
wariness after the motion of angels leads me.

Only a Memory . . .

desire
harsh
intentional
lee of moon's fracture

limb
bird-less

star
vacuity
her abstinence
pinch of wormwood
tinctured irony
sans laughter

Waiting

He:
You are the canon of Beatitudes
The litany of language of lust

She:
Hoary trident, half horse
Split between two heads
Janus brain jingo

He:
I ride the porpoise
plunging

She:
Heaven's halo
Forsaken
Truncated treasure
of birth deposits

He:
Sleepy

She:
Star company

He:
Moon drugged

She:
Into this cavity – out of this patience
Flowers bite off edges of time
Creation fat then flung to
the world of energy to nature's whim

He:
Must to battle
Rust to riches
Give me youth
Sword slung

She:
Peace is the ocean
I sit waiting
legs open
for doves

Help

I really could use your prayers
I have skin problems in layers
A mole is developing on my nose
My nails are curling on my toes
I have never forgave my neighbor
For keeping my Remington shaver
The immigrants over the back fence
have weeds that make gardeners wince
I could use a poem to feel better
My kids ignore me, nary a letter
The cemetery records went to pot
Caretaker deserted my parents plot
The Volvo needs a new clutch
I cannot drive it too much
It gets halfway down the street
and the radiator begins to heat
My wife sleeps in the TV room
In the chat page with "Bada Boom"
The dog pisses the entrance rug
The Hosta have holes from slugs

School reunion shut by the cops
I am too shaky to use my eye drops
My old hash pipe cracked in two
Marijuana got lost in an old shoe
I saw the parish priest at Great Clips
He was drunk and giving the girls tips
He is good friend to the Jewish Rabbi
Whose daughter is dating an Indian swami
Thirty years above her high school age
Has a parrot on his shoulder - an outrage
I promise to judge any poem you write
when I fix my modem later tonight

Moon

Do you see, sometimes, the same things as the moon?
I feel the pull of you into my words
watching the night pass.
There on the housetops comes a squint
of sun reflected.

This moon like layers of years between us.
Clever moon of remembrances of light senses skin.
Combination of moon -
sleepiness as remedies for time.
Hovering dollops, dot-by-dot connections,
night through.

Finding slippers, while you slept,
feet in shadows filtered.
Fingers of moments
arriving back to your unaware heaviness.

Is this moon a partner to the passing of life?
Can it take the place of separation from hope?

I cling to a pillow as sleep overcomes
prayers that you will be here when I wake,
unlike the moon.

Hurricane

These are the fringes
of tropical disturbances
as time suspended.
Drawing energy,
hunger, injustice
into the center.

Seizing solace in ocean
currents of tears, fears
of souls desiring redress.

Formed into massive swirls
of wind and moisture.

Awareness of
death and rebirth.

Bringing upsetting
reminders of natures
galactic whim.

Returning scenario
back switching
removing the shrapnel
I folded him into sheets
of unleavened bread
between layers of crushed
walnut, pistachio and honey.

Then when the mortars came back
smacking the perforated steel planking
I was safe inside a pin.

I heard words, "many are called. . . . . . . "
leaving the shallows of bone pits.

And, Wham! The self-propelled 155 went off
in my head and everywhere hell came down from
B52 silencers.

Celebrate

Buddha said: When you celebrate
you turn back into your heart
the beauty that came from others.

Adherent: But, my lord, if we
celebrate can we not be alone?

Buddha: A soul is never alone.
When moon pulses spread over
the land, it is the sun's celebration.

Adherent: Oh, wise one, is a celebration
a mirror?

Buddha: Gratitude from recognition is
of itself, the greatest form of celebration.
The soul that reaches heights can never
bask in its own aura's. The recognition
of self is like the layers of joy
surrounded by love from others.

Seasons

Lunisolar pentads, seasons clocking
rainy, dry, hurricane, tornado, wildfire
tropical, subtropical, locking, unlocking -
eternal divisions of wisdom and desire.

Rivulets and torrents in cloud wet springs
awakening grain and insects from sleep.
Clear and bright the fresh sun does bring
wishes of harvest that nature holds deep.

Hot the temperature starts grain in full.
The corn and alfalfa have acquired ears.
Summer solstice makes major heat lull
to ennui of laggard suspended careers.

Reaching further limits of white autumn dew
frost descends on church yards and streets.
Ambers, yellows, red to orange leaf hue.
Equinox suspension - false warmth retreats.

Abruptly flannels become famously vogue.
Windows slam shut, screens hide in uselessness.
Mild to major bone biting chill rouge,
Winter solstice cloaks all with its dress.

Karma aside, we are part of all nature's way.
We watch and fear powers of elemental kind.
Dalliances of differences keep depression at bay.
Life is a balance of change intoned to a daily grind.

Candy

Candy on Jefferson Avenue
in the sink-in seats of
the dark Vogue theater.

Candy with the forbidden
labels all over her body.

I told Michael Dennis Patrick Haag,
later, "She let me. I swear.
She let me kiss her. I touched
her, I swear. "

Michael: "No!"

Candy: "You don't know how lucky
you are, not being an orphan. "

(I was taken by surprise. Here I was with a normal family life. And she living in that big old house on East Grand Boulevard with all those kids having no other home of their own.)

Michael: "I bet you didn't. "

(Candy with the intoxicants of
a sixteen year old Goddess.
Those blue eyes. That short
blond hair. Those black flat
loafers and ankles of such
glorious artistic depictions.
Like some picture in the books
I skimmed in the library on
Saturday when no one else
knew what I was looking at.

Candy where are you now?
Fifty years later?
There was so much
I did not know, but,
my lips
still
remember. . . . .

Loose

the scented aroma of cinnamon
deliberate arms about me
a whisper of stillness
your lips imprinted
upon clove, cardamom

slight breeze
disturbing shadows
a mystery of the
lift of chemise
tantamount to desire

touch me to teach me
how to reach the supple
burnished tips of your
caramel eagerness

chalice preciousness
prismatic eyes

I find places where
silk smooths to skin
skin smooths to curvatures
graduating to sighs

You let me secret
private ceremonies
fingers arrested
repeated quivers

I am lost in this
cache of you
like a spilling
of juices of the moon on my lips

Language

ascending strata wisps of words
astral significances not heard
in a sows ear rhythm is blurred
clarified to enharmonic fifths
of Doppler shifts straight away

whisper to me of love
I am flimsing through
your eyes affected
only by my heart

signify with your flesh
the cutting away of
extraneous dogma

for you are the holy of holiest
given onto me the chalice
of your Eucharistic epistle

I am the conscious integrity

compromising touch with words
of Pantheon descendant journeys
into poetry of your lips

Soup

"To the Hebrides"
we two shall flee

"precious and amusing and unutterably bizarre"
we will take a taxi to a land diverse and far

where silliness is exposed to our reading eyes
certain Mr. Palmer who is rumored to have died

knock upon the door, Shakespeare waves to open
to Boswell in knickers eating snickers bars

the don, tenured to the afterlife by murder
leaves a trail of writings seeking solution

in the smoky circumlocution Nickleby wanders
while the Cheeryble brothers dance away

"The great man spoke. And we talked of me. "
many autumns the wild winds have set free

with usura hath no man a house. . . say Pound
hurry up please, it's time. . . . say T. S.

Inspector Field and a barmaid snitch
hats exchange, characters switch

and all in good fun

"But at my back I always hear
Time's winged chariot hurrying near. "

Entracte

Verwandlungsmusik stellung missionary
she's his pillow, an explosion to carry

dalliance delight skin skips loose
imagination at work he's her goose

we can position all intuition
into submission love's musician

hips, legs, arms entwined
lusty restraint bonds kind

love is note's ball of yarn
blending passion and charm

Reaching

Preamble - Prose:

Reaching out to be understood by others. In converse, we reach out to reach in to be understood by ourselves. There are deep collections of thought that beg for us to reach into. Ancient voices, poets, painters, spend time in company of their thoughts hoping for some new intrusion into their minds. We can only exist by reflection, as the moon teaches us:

Preamble - Poem:

I am scolded by the emptiness of space
but my companion, the sun, consoles me.

I am compromised by my self-centered humanity.
My companion, you, center me in objectivity.

This immeasurable vastness of dark matter
is companion to the compliments of stars.

This outpouring of words in so many idioms
begs for the judgment of true intellect.

Development:

I am the silent voice that follows human fears.
The spill of an echo of mountain lions tears.
I am the naked truth of a fire-less night.
Shadow of glinting eyes measured by fright.

To the entrance of my solitude conscious heart
I invite you to sit and help us make a start.

Musings:

My family from safety of limb branches
hails me in halls of stately stone mansions.

Could we but bridge the ancient longings
to redo injustice's blatant wrongings?

Words of Homer, Virgil, Shakespeare

give hope for all ages to hear.

Enharmonic:

That which is, was once to be
love I feel for all humanity
this danger of evil calamity
nature's callous polarity
cave to indifferent city.

We find solace in small spaces
hearts and hands, interlaces.

Breathe

First light crows
screech the air
settling silence.

Time frieze of
trees, birds,
air become
blue draped
mountains touching
clouds in joy.

Halo's of lovely
circles your eyes
to scrolls of
ancient texts
along your breasts
as you measure
the heart in
sleeping breaths.

Notice

world newness
Caravaggio deviant

deprivation
getting skinny

synthetic logic
regime cyberpunk
steampunk

itch claw spider
  Karincoma
    slinking
      web weave
        sklunch

Innocence

We turn to trees
as legends decree
inside leaves
faeries weave.

A melon moon
lace pantaloons
tiny cup of tea
chair bumblebee.

Awning of mist
invitation list
a teddy bear
ribbon in hair.

Time's cessation
pure creation
angels circle
child miracle.

There is no sin
in our heaven
only profusion
star's illusion.

Credo

Vamprisses awake to take
your place with fangs of intuition.

Below the desire of men driven
we drive desire into their imaginations,
clever creatures of our own invention.

Break the sensitivity of skin for
we love brute
oh! how we love the spent force of empty emotion
for below the surface we are calm and in control.

Drink from our cup the moon's envy
the white chalice brimmed with embryonic blood.

Drink, we take in and release all creation.

Drink, our bodies are hurricanes never spent.

Animus

Preamble:

The first animal is human.
Preconception, morality,
inhumanity—are a few of the
differences dividing it from
all other forms of animals.

It is the first because it can
reflect upon itself and history.

Awareness of spirit world was diminished
when God gave humans free will. Here is
why: Humans cannot think about choices
while staying in tune with all levels of
reality at the same time. We cannot serve
two masters.

All other animal types must conform
to the dictates of their limitations

but without fear of death.

In some magical way, all animals
are in contact with all forms of life
around them.

We humans can only respect the
power of all creation as a humbling
force that diminishes our ego and
makes us thankful to be part of a
mystery too large for us to understand,
but a mystery that we must strive to
understand as much as we possibly can.

Poem:

I am the spark of the wolf's eye
crack of silence from eagle's cry
bend of the giraffe neck so high
lovely filament of the butterfly

come upon me red cardinal branch
deer so shy only seen by chance
the fireflie's dusk-to-dark dance
white crane bobbing mouth lance

upon the dolphins back I ride
inside Queen Anne Lace I hide
spider has me bound and tried
snake coiled or silent glide

these creatures seek no praise
to heaven their natures raise
we are tied to love in days
unconscious in so many ways

Jaded

In love with the siren call
decrying insecurity
carillon tolling need.

Besiege me women:
soft curves
steel nerves
sex allures.

Hopeless searching of eyes.

Odysseus roped to the mast.
Aeneas swooning in Dido's cave.
Zeus mesmerized by Hera.
Agamemnon needing Clytemnestra.
Menelaus captivated by Helen.

More than jaded - satiated
in your eyes, ladies
lost - your slave.

Still it is you I love
despite the searching,
in war, men die crying
for their mother.

The scintillating sway
as she walks away
drives me crazy.

Put me away
for insanity
for the female.

Crane

Remember the white crane
in the protected pond between
the Home Depot and distant houses?

Soon the delivery trucks will stop
Winter will slow everything, but the
browned Glyceria ,Typha, Shave Grass
will remain as a reminder of summer.

The crane, its crook neck and ungainly
movements like time photography, will
endure Drakes and fat belly Canadensis.

It will reject the noise of traffic
and airplanes and smell of fast food
colliding around its eating waters.

And slight movements of temperate air
will pass around it as it stays frozen
on its stick legs all winter, immobile

and breathing very infrequent like a
frog patient in the rigid ice.

As I drive by each day to say hello
to this phenomenal friend of mine,
I will thank him for giving me you.

Psalm of Moon

Whistled hoops in calico pinto
Calliope of sun's severability
"Sing the mark" of female fertility,
history of love's logo.

Take me to the Ferris wheel, lord,
dizzy with the lunar lovers
circled by the diffidence
of haws and harriers romance.

Master ring leader, whip
snip-snap, keeps façade alive
of ancient eclipsed eyes.

Psalm of the infant
Come upon swaddled sweetness
precious temperaments
wafts of crushed lavender
floating dust powder dew
mobile of filleted glass filaments.

When my soul was lifted
it was at the urgency of your giggles,
the unquenched joy of
practicing fingers, toe squirms.

Your eyes, yet attached to ethereal realms,
still see the aura's of angelic hosts.

Psalm of Yearning

Into the emptiness of my heart
spill your balm of empathy.

Strengthen the walls of my refuge,
Lord of the great and the lowly.

When the few, you have found favor with,
misunderstood the depth of your mysteries,
tear, oh Lord, the pages from the tomes of heaven.
Remove the sanctity of wisdom from your books.

Please, my holy one, you spoke and no ears heard.
You moaned from the anterooms of mansions of sorrow.
When the shadows of centuries leaned in the windows
and left their dust upon the shelves of ancient pages,
you wept at the futility
of plentitude of nonsensicalness.

Bring me to a culvert of peace.
Enclose me with breadth, depth of seasons.
Hide me in the furze and fern of tree circles.

Empty my soul of ego and shriveled dreams.

I am a vacuous compartment of your will, oh spirit of such spaciousness.
Come into this rectified sanctum of dim reverence to your holy hosts.
Bolster me to face the leftover images
of a world in chaos.

Psalm for Mrs. Haag

There were three things
lurking about the dim room:
death, life and sorrow.

Mrs. Haag lay in her makeshift bed
where the couch was removed.

Mr. Haag filled the room with his
patience and care for her in his
quiet wise way:
(One day the neighbor's dog scared me.
Mr. Haag talked slow to him and reached
between the fence as the dog let his
ears be rubbed. "Try it", he told me.)

Michael Dennis Patric Haag lost his mother
to cancer.

"Why did your family leave Ireland, Michael?"

Three things ate my teenager heart that year:
death, life and sorrow.

As the Buddha learned, I learned how death smelled.
I learned that life is cloudy with history untold.
And the deep channels, still with me, of the sorrow
of people I love dying and living.

Take me to the empty spaces, Lord, where the tears
will fill the drought and sun light the dark.

Give those,
who filter through the shadows and disappear,
solace.

Psalm for Anna (leaf/ leaves)

tree buds burst
air sucked back

wink lashes of time

rented

her arrival spun tongues

villagers

disappointed at her sex

many hands would be needed
to feed her - men's

then this switch - like miracles
a basket, found in the woods
full of autumn

unleashed mellow across the land

sometimes God lets things
fall before the seasons fade

and she swung the blacksmith's hammer
silencing the peasants
who needed
to walk
through
the waist high chestnut
leaves
all year long
    to get to her shop

Psalm of Friendship

In Tiffany tallow
invitational chairs
quiet speciousness
draws you to me -
my special prayer.

Slip the pages slowly
of the shadowed years
collected between us
sprinkled joyous tears.

Open ended destinies,
you the garden
me the trees
we the harvest
heaven's fief.

Psalm for a Bird

Dredge the pond sludge.
Upbraid the heaven's gateways to the slime sluice.
Call the night witches to stir the sediment of stone.
And out of the crevices in breathless gasps
pull the crabs and crayfish out of their sleep
with unmerciful siphons of jiggers
stabbed by the yellow beaked daggers
of the stilted steady tottering
white hungry crane.

Psalm of Patricia

So many years I prayed.
After enlistment in battle I was left crying.
After marriage, so hastily entered into,
became the interminable unending retreat.

I cried unto the Lord from the deepest part of my soul.
I falter and stumble over experience
that others find easy.

I spoke to the void in hopes of visions of awareness.

Aromatic spirits of musty cleverness
descend upon me.
Ceremonial frankincense, enter my hearts chambers.
Fill me with balm of a mighty queen's
minted camphor.
Clear the doubtful misgivings with secret fragrances.

Out of the pitch blindness in one magic moment
a door opened, you standing, me falling immediately
into your arms, spilling years of tears that emptied
my misgivings immediately as if a healing miracle.

At last the person resurfacing me into life.

A friend forever not a hastily chosen wife.
Stalker of hidden paths in nature's mysteries
hidden behind semblance of bowers of eaves.
How the years have tumbled into our pouches
touchstones smooth from our finger touches.

Psalm of Passing

She opened all the windows
sent the torn pages of the Quran
flittering into the blinding white.

In the soft shoes of silence
turning from the tribe of Thamud
she was floated to the gateway.

Hallelujahs shook the halls of empyrean.

Skin shedding crochet colors
wrap-like comfort layered gowns,
the attendant tailors of angels
clasped her waist in gold ribbon.

Gloria in Excelsis Deo.
Praise thundered as firmament
risen to stupendous heights.

"Come my daughter of dutifulness,

place your finger on the script
read your treasured deeds. "

She always knew that judgment
would find favor with her
and the reassurance overwhelmed
her into a dream of soul-sleep.

Psalm of Mary Haag

Husband and I left Ireland
came to this crazy street
where birds were different
there was no bog or peat.

Neighbors brought casseroles
horses have asphalt feet
night crickets are all dead
no ocean, all cement heat.

He works in a factory
sis in a bakery sweet
the cancer, we were told
will run its course complete.

Breasts fed two children
hurt, I grit my teeth
drugs make me sleepy
mind seems to retreat.

Oh furze and moss roadways
beaten down paths replete
trees overhanging shadows
hearts that keep calm beat.

The history of Patrick
priest whose eyes meet
every Sunday sermons
pews straight and neat

Take me back please
death please greet
Eire emerald island
Clare county seat.

Jigging the Twist

Gigging polyamory, bodacious Salt Lake jim-jam.
One: A sliver hippy ma-munch-ca-pa.
She got ear for ringtone
gigong easy mouse potato.

Drama queen filling in the big box
with the hip hop.
I, doing an ollie on the skip board
with the wave pool.

She say: "My mano got a soul patch,
but he aint no coqui. "

Drawing in the unibrow
bypass the gastric silent:
"Sheesh!"

Cause, all things aeriform ignescent expire.
And we skittle down to the lunch-scrunch
with la la love.

Extended Thoughts

Life copies life.
History repeats in a dwindling haze of remembrance.

High culture came from minds that left patterns
that we all agree are original models:

Bach, Michelangelo, Darwin, Shakespeare -
this is high culture.

We can easily label ourselves watered down, thin,
weak attempts that never rise to the level of
the past.

Maybe the reason
we are the way we are
is because
there is too much information around
which we attempt
to wrap our minds around when we, as poets, write.

I have, at various times, amassed books, records, paintings in such magnitude as to create envy in the thoughts of the ancients that worked with much thinner information.

Maybe there is a theory at work:
The more information available, the less chance
of reaching the watermarks of high culture.

Maybe, there is no more large culture to invent.

Maybe we can take a lesson from Science: The fact that nature as it unfolds in accepted patterns, reaches a point where all the patterns have been discovered and are in place.

There are no more rainbows
can compete with the first
that greeted Eden skies.

There are no more words
to rise to the level of
a simple alphabet or surpass it.

Healing

I cover myself in dusty down
beneath the heaven's mists.

When I was a libertine -
I beg your forgiveness,

for the quick emotion
taken at your expense.

The youthful fiber
energy to waste.

Collisions of time
turn the mind inward.

And the secrets of the past
become the shame of eyes
softly praying in rusty wishes
of your enfolding heart.

I am not hungry
the widow that feeds me
is sustained by her faith
her son is reborn

Ahab gambles
Jezebel smirks
famine descends upon the land

the wicked advance
the anger of God
descends to altars
of desire

come into my cave
I have preached
been heard
by God of good.

here on the path
a chariot lifts me
past my enemies
peace settles
in flat stillness

the widow is dead
as her son
my cave is empty
Ahab and Jezebel
become Fables

my deeds
enter history
on chariots
of fury

Canticle of Comedy

Accelerating soul arrived
upon the earth into the womb
linking life of one who died
blossoming outside the tomb.
The child yet to be groomed
to stand and stumble daintily
to sin and pray so saintily.

And oh how life did burn the log,
marriage, divorce no breaking ranks
vocation, station a lowly frog
bills, spills and empty banks.
Children who grew with no thanks
Friends few, no psychology
Life a dry misery.

WITH lullay, lullay, like a child,
Thou sleepèst too long, thou art beguiled!

"My darling dear, my daisy flower,
Let me," quoth he, "lie in your lap. "
"Lie still," quoth she, "my paramour,
Lie still hardily1, and take a nap. "
His head was heavy, such was his hap,
All drowsy, dreaming, drowned in sleep,
That of his love he took no keep,
With hey, lullay, etc.

With ba, ba, ba, and bas, bas, bas!
She cherished him both cheek and chin
That he wist never where he was;
He had forgotten all deadly sin!
He wanted wit her love to win:
He trusted her payment and lost all his pay;

She left him sleeping and stale2 away,
With hey, lullay, etc.

The rivers rough, the waters wan;
She sparèd not to wet her feet.
She waded over, she found a man

That halsèd3 her heartily and kissed her sweet;
Thus after her cold she caught a heat.
"My lief,4" she said, "rowteth5 in his bed;
Iwys6 he hath an heavy head,"
With hey, lullay, etc.

What dreamest thou, drunkard, drowsy pate?
Thy lust and liking is from thee gone;
Thou blinkard blowboll7, thou wakèst too late;
Behold thou liest, luggard, alone!
Well may thou sigh, well may thou groan,
To deal with her so cowardly.
Ywis, pole-hatchet,8 she blearèd thine eye!
Quoth Skelton Laureate.

Dying

Compact little beads on a stringer
spilling out of an untied end
into random motion silently
bouncing off of giggling clouds.

Heavy fist athletic Pantheon gods
peeling onions with rain collecting
into lagoons around their eyes of
bluish moons - down straggly beards.

Embellished ocean horizons of emptiness.
Whispers of strands of palm leaves
stark to the immobility of shore birds.

Halos - street lights - electric alleluias.
Cordons of reverent pizzicato plucks
in lower registers of memories.

You holding my hand as

happiness reaches deep.
monuments to beauty
I am a thing that thinks.
I am a thing of beauty.

The cries of Ilium's dying
at the hands of the Greeks,
interests me not.

I do not see Aeneas
when I shave.

I see a collection of thoughts
that are only mine.

I refuse to share them with you
because you would not understand.

The sliding of a confection
sugar white moon in licorice space

full of star speckles -

That is my reflection of beauty that
I chose to keep for myself.
You can buy your own box of Ju Ju's.
When the soldiers came with their boots
resonating against the wooden doors, I
answered, "No one lives here. Take my
neighbors to your camps. "

Beauty protected me as I brushed my teeth.

I love myself.

I can only blink at references to
histories of ugliness where the vortex
whirled in a gyration of meaninglessness.

If, perchance, you put me in a lime pit
where the splinters of broken bones still

contain the freshness of torn muscle and
ligaments, all covered with sticky mucus,
or drying blood, mixed with dust and twigs,
well, I will scream to your bayoneted eyes:
I am beautiful, even as you fade before me .

Bring Me Hope

The escaping light refreshes itself in spaces
between stars
where aspirants contend with words thrown here
and there
like horseshoes without a stake to catch them.

I search the pinpoints of the burnished ends
of long gone
heavens. I scan the heads resting
on sleepy pillows of history.

Here in my pocket is a penny found tail-up.
Here is a piece of paper lost
from a cash register roll forever.

Here is some lint.

Did you think that I was waiting
for a hole to happen in my pocket?
No, I am waiting for another
windmill of words to gyrate out of my head.
And, bingo, a snippet of sounds
emerges into a special brand of consumer goods.

Tell the afternoon sun that day is caught
in Autumn mists.

Wish for the tree limbs to bend
beneath the cardinal's feet.
Say a special prayer for the grey/black crane
at pond's edge.

Tell the geese that their games will soon
be ended
in flight.

For all the world waits for the drama
of a shifting in winds
when the collars, mufflers
and gloves will conceal fragility.

And, we,
the poets will blanche at the space left for us to live,
sharpen our wits so as to begin a new chemistry
of love.

New

You have driven yourself to the edge of irrelevance
and we now hold your vapid power up for ridicule.

Your industrial de-evolution has cycled itself out.
The factories of fashion are empty and silent tombs.

We have bourne our Beauvoirs, Epinays, Deffands and Brontes, into your parlors of patriarchy, stretched upon biers.

Climates of mysterious atmospheres invent the dawn.
The fragments of an old Pantheon have disassembled.

Anecdotes of your heroes have lost pace
with our hearts.
We drive your insecurities into side shows of history.

We are the new women to your faint obscurities.

Silence

Mind is a catch basin for all differing realities.
The consciousness exists first inside memories.
From the large spacious present of all eternity
we sense existence overlapping all that we see.

The Gods have given us special select free will
to restrain ourselves or take more than our fill.
We are sacred seed from ground others till.
Born of dreams, desires with love to spill.

The beating of our hearts to the sparrow's pulse.
The falcon's descent shot to the quarry grouse.
The red tail hawk finding a city street mouse.
The kingfisher screaming wanting fish to arouse.

These harmonies and destinies of life all abound
from our soul to spheres of nature in the round.
We are born of earth and leave dust to the ground.
A mystery of sun, water, air, silence of sound.

Coincidence of Cloistered Kisses

you and me
under a tree
eternity
put on hold
  for love
    to blossom
        over and over

Abounding

We derive from the scrunch
expounding splendor
semblance of curiosities
empathetic angels
Gods

possibilities: cheery , dreary, sluggish or sad

in the morning when the big book is trundled
onto the dais, the bespectacled choristers harrumph

singing of our deeds of greatness to match
the slinging of tapered mountains
dissolving into sky or sea

we are florescence
seeded to glory
munificent
exponentially explosive

deliberated over centuries
shuffled at random
chancy bits of life

Away

I sit on the clefts of memories.
Torrents of emotion spill away.
Giddiness for love was yesterday.
Emptiness replenishes constancy.

Thirty years of loving one person
has been more than any expectations
that the past could have foretold.

Still to come is the decline and decrepitude
that nature give us as a rounding out of wisdom.

Remembering the words read that attention
of the soul focuses on some new reality
and the pain of a body dying is eased
by the absent consciousness escaping
the physical mind.

When we are born, we jump into escape
from the grand spaciousness of all

into the tight needs of the infant
crying for instants of food, comfort,
air, taste, sights of new life.

When we die we expand into multiplicity.

It is easy to see how life diverts our attention.

If I love you it is because you are
imposing yourself over my over-soul.

You are the grand escarpment that
keeps me temporarily comforted.

When you die I only have myself to face
in the beauty of balance
in the crush of everlasting
in the pull of memory
away from my own decline.

Owl

I am here as an emissary of humanity.
I can only sit in the benches and attempt to translate
the few incidences where language and desire overlap.

Sliding the door wall quietly
so as to not disturb the wind chimes,
I slip onto the patio and sit gently
on the dew covered plastic chair.

Upon the fifth branch of the lonely tree surviving in the space between houses, an owl sits, barely visible by the light of an October cloud draped moon.

At four in the morning, I listen to several owls,
distant -
woo woo wooing each other.

I presume they woo woo for communication?
Or maybe for survival if any of them spot food?
Maybe they woo woo to position themselves in quadrants where they judge space so as to canvas as large an area as possible for the group as a whole?

There is a distant hum of street traffic,
sparse in the early morning.
There is the cold silence of
sleepy house windows, all shuttered.
There is the lovely twinkle of stars
between the jaggedly scattered clouds.

The sound of the cat purring,
the barking of a dog, the chirp of a bird,
the slight movement of
your head on the pillow as you acknowledge

my hand upon your soft flesh beneath the flannel,
the woo woo that comes out of
your mouth as you continue sleeping,
this magic of a language foreign to me:
I can only translate as love and I am humbled.

Raptor Accipitiridae

Earth is an uneven line
day and darting shadows.
Spindled arms,
slinged frustum-like funnels
in which we navigate.

Float drifting bubbles
warm uplifts
tottered views.

Telescope surveying
movement against gray surfaces.

Absolute letting go of all
sustaining horizons.

A divestment of gravity.
Bolt shot of feathers and
lightness directed
in fixation at a prey.

We become the chorus
of the ancient echoes.

The eye swift to the skull
depressions emptied of all hope.

The General's Genitals

Nobuko was unforgiving. If anyone crossed her she loosened her tongue freely.

The one time she proved her worth was when the General showed himself, without his Aide, outside the door to Sarge's office, wrapped in a skimpy towel.

On previous overnight billeting, the General had complained about the pipes expanding, the room being too cold. So, this trip everything was carefully readied.

The Sarge called Nobuko, his voice echoing down the corridor.

When she was told that there was no soap in the General's shower she exploded with cursing. She marched up to the second floor with the General and Sarge rushing behind her, trying to keep up with her pace.

She stormed past the Aide de Camp, who was smoking a cigar in his shorts in a chair. She did not hesitate. The Aide scrambled to get his pants. Nobuko swung the shower door open, pulled back the curtain to the window and lifted a full bar of wrapper soap off the ledge.

Sarge snuffled. Nobuko handed it with force to the General who, forgetting himself, reached to accept the soap, allowing the towel to drop to the floor.

Nobuko took one short look at the naked general, sneered, and stormed out of the room continuing to swear evenly but smiling as she walked.

Clutch

just to replace the plate
start at the differential,
all the way back
rear wheels on a jack

loosen, remove the shaft bolt
holding each rear shock -
pull them out of the coil spring

next, remove the pinion on
the geared transverse module
which, of course, allows the tires
to turn from a opposite spin

(Positrak?)

good!

lay the, now released, axle shaft on the ground
at the back of the bell-housing remove the hex nuts
holding the octagonal cover to the gear assembly

(We certainly hope you have drained the case.)
i did. don't worry

pull the drive shaft away from the transmission
cover throwout collar interface connector catch

disconnect the pedal linkage
check for play in the swivel joints
if you need to replace the linkage
have your wife call Tom to see if he is free
to take you to Spade's Auto Parts on seven mile
remember: they close at six

"Stop. Take a break. "

keep the kids away from under
the back of the car

if your water breaks,
Tom will have to take you to the hospital

"My water is not going to break. Sheesh.
The doctor said
I have two weeks, yet. "

the lemonade is excellent.

"Thanks. You didn't touch the cookies. "

i would like to touch you

"Fix the car, banana head. "

unscrew the large tranny unit
pull it
drop it

examine the flywheel driving member surface
(If it needs grinding, you got problems.)
(Someday you will be able to afford a new car.)
yea!

replace the pressure plate. make sure
it is aligned to the throwout bearing
slotted into the the housing cover

see that it meshes correctly
when the engine is firing and
activating the assembly through
the transmission interface

reassemble the whole package in reverse
you know how she hates when you curse

Joy

arch of
eye stitched
silent coffin
dissolving
head
above reason
 lips
letting go a simple
flowered gravity
exploded
my serenade

Indigenous

heart severed from   heaven
bundled woven memories
places child's fervor
rivers as days
nights as birds
of exploding myths

i miss u so
that got old
comes up
see
you on
paper
moon crushed
into powder
smiles for
the frames
dresser top days
An equally believable story of creation

Prayer of Mission

Dear aspirants, more but, lessor of angelic space,
Into thy hands I offer all in me of grace.
I strip myself of dishonor,
Lay my soul open to
All that is good,
Never erase
Your love.

I start my mission in privacy
But public to your host
Where decency
Becomes all
Prayer.

Prayer of Cleansing

Where all harshness of heavy thoughts
Spills out of my dreams
Making me to light
As if a bird
A Breeze

I try the patience of season's girth -
A robe of change accustomed
To silence of ice
Clamor of spring
Airless summer
Autumn's change

Your Face Has Wisdom To It.

Tell me, how do you account for
the difference between Freud and Jung?
Freud believes that all psychosis derives from the natural world or environment or the influence of the consciousness from the time of birth.
Jung believes in archetypes that are formed
on a level before birth.
B. F. Skinner was a modern proponent of Freud. B. F. Skinner wrote the famous book on raising children, "Verbal Behavior".
Noam Chomsky is a modern proponent of Jung's theory of preset archetypes. He is a living philosopher and very outspoken leader of thought that leans toward conservative. He is considered one of the greatest new thinkers of our age.
These two theories form the basis of human psychosis in this way: Either we are born without preconception or we exist before birth.
Sorry for throwing this at you. I am a person who is either totally silly or totally serious.

(The following are emails written to various women met online at dating sites. I have changed the names for obvious reasons. –Editor)

Scriabin, Einstein, and Mrs. Tolstoy

Hello. I watched you pull up in the parking lot with the yellow car and I knew, right away, that I wanted to talk to you. You were driving my cousins stolen antique Ford woody station wagon and I am sure that you bought it from "Ace Used Cars" around the corner from the Unitarian Church where Tibor played piano on Sunday after services. Sometimes I hate Tibor, because he thinks he knows how to play the Liszt Transcendental Etude and he does not. If he would only take the time to listen to a CD recording of it by a known pianist, then he would realize that his tempo and rhythms are all off. I do not particularly like Liszt because he was a womanizer and he did not age gracefully. More important, his music seems too stilted to me. I prefer more emotional composers who write from the heart, such as Scriabin. Alexander Nicholas Scriabin died at age thirty six in Switzerland from a boil on his lip. Rubenstein told his mother that she should let him play piano at home without being admitted to the Conservatory. Rubenstein assured his mother that Scriabin, who hated to follow lessons, would do better without formal instruction. This proved true, and Scriabin wrote some of the most beautiful music all on his own. Scriabin died in a room with a young violinist that he was having an affair with in Switzerland. I sometimes think that these affairs that people have are more important than their marriages. Gauguin died with natives in the islands while his wife tried to raise his children without his support or presence. Now, Tolstoy's wife was kind of smart. She told Leo to go travel (probably to get him out of her way).

Madame Tolstoy rewrote "War And Peace" about seven times till she got his novel where she finally gave it to a publisher in polished form. Madame Tolstoy ran, with great efficiency, the large estate that she and Leo owned with all the servants. She, in her way, was a more powerful force than her husband. Same situation with Einstein's wife, who contributed (with no credit) the largest portion of the famous paper presented to the scientific community on Time and Relativity. Probably the greatest theory that any human being in history ever developed. Relativity, in a very clear fashion, affirmed reincarnation. Lot of people do not know this, and you, as the driver of a stolen car, probably do not either. I would suggest you look on the bottom metal tab near the base of the windshield on the driver's side and tell me if there is a Vehicle Identification Number scratched off with a metal instrument. I am going to wait till you go to Sunday services at the Baptist Church on Fourth and Simpson Drive, near the Baldinger's Pet Supply. I will stand in the window near the parrot cages and watch you park and go inside with your Centennial Bible tucked under your arm. Then I will sneak over and hot wire the Woody and drive it to my cousin's garage and give it back to him. There, now you have some of my thoughts and you can do what you wish with them.

Potential Date:

You are a very pleasing looking person. I wish I could say the same about me. Children in buggies in grocery store lines, cry when they see me. Dogs bark, it rains every day, cars honk, lottery numbers go out of their way to avoid winning tickets I find on the ground in parking lots. It is a real rum-go for me. I was born the son of a butcher. I cut my finger every time I butter my toast. I have the most terrible relationships with people and all seven of my wives line up sequentially in my driveway to steal my newspaper or write on my garage door with magic marker. The police wait for my car to ticket me. My rabbi uses me as an example of heavenly retribution. At sports events, vendors spill beer on me. I did my astrological chart and found out that I was descended from a line of char people who never went to high school. I insist that you do not answer this email because I would have nothing to say to you. I am using google/word/dictionaries and an old ratted bible as source documents for this writing. I am well aware of intuition abilities except I never get any internal messages other than when my electricity goes out for not paying my monthly bill. I do tax returns, as a CPA, at home, after selling my practice to my partners. I love classical music but my neighbors play rap all day out of their open windows. I get tired of do-wop. I get tired of Chopin - can you imagine? John Field composed rat-a-tat-tat. Beethoven composed while eating snap-crackle-pop cereal. Shostakovitch composed in a funk. Why the hell he dug in and stayed in Russia to be abused for his musical ideas, is probably an example of simple obstinacy. Einstein never gave his wife credit for co-authoring the great theory of time/space continuum. I always remembered some college teacher describing the theory of relativity as: "If you sit on a hot stove with the woman you love, you never feel the heat. " What rubbish. I have burns on my bottom from trying it.

What else can I tell you? I write poetry that everyone hates. Here's an example:

Better that the ordinary
cross your days ornery
and sticky buns never do
petrol breath follows you

See what I mean? Stay away from me. I paid for this Harmony stuff in hopes that I will never find a woman who understands me. Here is my profile:

curmudgeon smudgeon
aint never budging
born sign of the skunk
walks with a clunk

I love long walks on short piers
I have star memories rampant
on cloudy nights damp

What are you doing on the helm of a boat? You look so magazinish like you was posing with your hands - I bet pirates tied you to the mast? If I tried to save you with my sword, I would be run-through with the cutlass of a dirty sailor.

You are wearing pantaloons like a seafarer? Your hair is blowing in the mist.

Here is what you are saying to the TV cameras: I denounce America and all its Yiddish yaps / all its Christian claps. I embrace Allah. I make a pilgrimage to Hawaii to pray to the great pineapple princess who never was and never will be.

enough silliness.

Please take none of this serious.

Dear Sally:

1 - there is something about your direct words that strike me.
2 - I challenge you to one simple poem in return for this email:
3 - one simple poem from me:

"Cat's Activities"

I wake as a reminder - Sunday is gone.
More - Monday means this:
work and sober.
Not that drunk was
but weekends are like my cat:
oblivious to work.

About this cat: What a deal, huh?
He wakes without reminders: per-se.
He wakes only to guide himself on my attention.
He intrudes, demands, interrupts, diverts my
activities so as to squeeze in an affectionate
neck rub or so.

So, I wake and wish that (she, you) someone was
here to spill like shadows across my carpets;
to intersperse themselves between my activities
with obviated intentions of keeping me from
the obvious and including me in their version of love.

you have a warm and kind face.
as a writer, do you struggle with clarity? historical reality gets very clouded with indigenous differences.
as an avid reader, a fact held me: That Virgil wrote fictitious characters and plots.
history often ignores that Hitler and Stalin were responsible for over fifty million deaths each.

history often misses the fact that Hitler built over 30 thousand concentration camps to hold the captives that indecently were described as less than human or less than Aryan.

Most of those captives probably went insane before they died. The hallmark of those camps were lack of air, heat, facilities, water, windows, food, medicine - lack of every kind of decency as well as the total degradation of human spirit.

It is beyond my understanding how a large group of people can be swayed by history, even when it is too base to be called anything but a total miscalculation of human endeavor. Even the word evil seems too tame for some of our histories.

It is funny to me how opera always has the heroine dying. History is a series of wars that cull the women and children first and foremost. This is just a small bit of talk in hopes that you do not get turned off by my directness.
I very much like your face.

I just watched *"The Curious Case of Benjamin Button"* and here were my thoughts:
F. Scott Fitzgerald was a genius of a writer. Such an intricate story line with all his characters developed so well, made the movie come alive and interesting.

I judge a movie by how well I am carried away from my normal thoughts and reactions. This movie was one of the best I have seen in a long time. I was left wishing for more of the story to keep me so interested.

I particularly liked the "intersecting" idea of characters aging in reverse or forward and reaching a point where they match each other so well at a particular age and state of mind. It is here that we or they seem to have the best learning criteria.

I like the idea that relationships can maximize the depth that each person can reach because conditions between them make perception and understanding come alive.

I have found that all my deep relationships in my life have been as such: conditions made it right for either myself or the other person to learn the most about themselves and add to their genuine soul.

Please, I hope I have been clear and tell me what you think?

Dear Philomena:

I am so heartened by your smile and your email response.

As an English Composition/Poetry/Play writing concentrated major in college, I have used my writing skills to win most of my tax cases in my profession of being a CPA, over the years.

I continue to write poetry -

The lovely and intricate details of emotion/plot or of the action/characters/scenes of the Great Gatsby are reminiscent, to me, of the rich depth of Dostoevsky's writings such as "Brothers Karamazov".

I think that the Gatsby story, almost like grand opera, cloaks itself in sad wasting of life's opportunities by the characters. The winding web of conflicting emotion of each character, makes the reader believe that some overwhelming force (like an ocean) carries each character along unwittingly.

I truly believe that F. Scott Fitzgerald and his Zelda - each consumed by literature, alcohol and their need for love and recognition - mirror the books and themes they portrayed within their writing.

Fyodor Dostoevsky's life of suffering at the hands of poor health and political constraints, sets the pace of his novelistic characters.

The thing that makes Gatsby/Karamazov/Hemmingway's characters and all great literary characters so interesting is the depth and intricacies that their lives depict. Good writers can weave their main characters into such detailed extensions in their lives. We, as readers, get such rewards from these composite sketches of fiction mimicking real life.

Only just last week I was quickly reading through a book that came into my hands by accident: "The Nick Adams Stories". Hemingway's first stories about his growing up in upper Michigan in the Traverse City region near the "Big Three Heart River" area, where I spent some time years ago.

Only just last week I read in one of the Nick Adam stories how a character, who was indebted to a doctor in the town, created an argument with the doctor. The doctor, in talking to his friend, states that his patient feels guilty about owing the money to him and, thus, as a defense mechanism, creates an argument with the doctor as a way of having an excuse for not paying him.

As a CPA I have had the exact same situation with some clients over the years, where they will not pay me and use the excuse of the emotional argument that arose between us, as a way of not paying me. Amazing! Here is fiction mirroring real life.

These insights and discoveries are what I enjoy the most about reading or any endeavor that awakens me to new perceptions.

Hope you do not mind the rambling.

Dear Philomena 2:

I thank you so much for your attention and wisdom in talking to you. Many good wishes to you. And, I hope to hear that you will continue to write to me of anything that interests you.

To My Fantasy, Florence:

You have a lovely wise, pleasant look about you in your two pictures. Visually, you are the nicest of all the many persons I have seen on Match and Harmony.

This process is so new to me and I am making a lot of mistakes being as wordy as I am. I am this loquacious and extemporaneous in all things in my life. So much so that: wearing heart on my sleeve is an understatement.

I have just ended a thirty five year relationship and I am very much missing doing things with a lady, buying things for her, thinking of ways to please her, like flowers or special things that I know she will like. Like buying her stamps or surprising her with little things I find in walking the aisles of stores. I do not think I can live without doing these things. Right now, I have been doing this for my sister, whom I love. She is married to a chemical engineer and they live about fifty miles from me. I buy her lamps, knitting supplies, candy, and her husband eats it all.

I am a cpa who has about 200 clients I work on in my second bedroom. I sold my practice to my partner and kept the lovely clients that were so special to me. Working alone, I make more money that I ever made running a full office of staff over the years.

"Jontoue" was part of a litter of alley kittens in Detroit. She lived with me for fourteen years and died in my arms. It took two years to grieve her out of my heart. She was named by a friend who had to give her up as a small kitten. I kept the name out of courtesy to him, and the name became commonplace and irreplaceable. "Master Percy", a rescue cat, became her replacement. I named him after the knight of the round table that discovered the holy grail. "Master Percy" is the most gentle, playful cat I have ever known. I cannot be without him. He is never allowed out of my house.

I live in a high ceiling condo with much privacy. My neighbors are friendly but hardly see me. I have plants everywhere.

They are beautiful and I trim/transplant/arrange and love them. My small garden in the allowed area is praised. My past years gardens that I disbanded when I moved here, filled over thirty plots around where I used to live. One of my most missed and favorite plantings was the orchid called "Queen of the Night". Tall and purple standing above a spreading plot of short purple orchids, she used to call to me in my sleep outside my window.

I talk a lot. I type faster than I can talk. I think faster than I can talk and I am very lazy. Years ago I used to do triathlons. Now I vegetate.

You probably will read this and wipe your brow out of endurance. I have only told you a little of the junk I talk about. I think that my uncles were lucky because they were heroes of world war II and when I came back from a year in Viet Nam - no one really cared. I married and divorced and drifted and passed the CPA exam and have never remarried because I am afraid of women, but not too afraid of them that I won't flirt at a distance and do things for them. All the ladies I know adore me because I am solicitous and harmless. I believe most men are afraid of women but will never admit it. Women have the patience of a flower unfolding. Men have the patience of an angry buffalo.
Damn, I can't stop writing. I am looking at your picture as I write. I type over 200 words a minute

without any mistakes. I am a writer. I have won most all of my tax cases because of my ability to write. I can write a poem like:

And the colors of the sky dim to gray
as night ends it's conference with day
talking real fast with the moon at bay
and the silly stars giggling so far away

I have only just ended a thirty five year relationship with a woman who started out as a spiritual adviser and became my best friend all these long years. I fit myself into her marriage by promising her husband to never have sex with her and never offend him. The three of us became companions on hikes, dinners, museum trips, parties every week. I allowed them to keep me distant from their family and as they got cancer and Parkinson's disease respectively, they slowly eliminated me from the arrangements they made to die. She is, no doubt, a strong woman. Her insistence to her husband, kept me intertwined. I also allowed her to dominate me because I felt she was helping me, and to a large extent, I became a whole person because of her. The only drawback being that my unconditional generosity and love were not enough in the face of her impending fate.

Lately, I have been very lonely without a special person to call and discuss all the things that go on in my life. I do not think I can live without that need being filled again. I like being alone, but I need a connection that is as deep as one can get. Sex is totally irrelevant. Intimacy is not.

Your name is Consuela. I like that.

My name is Michael and I hate it when people call me Mike. Mike is for a boxer or a butcher. My dad was a Mike. His driver's license said so, too. My dad boxed and was a butcher all his life. He and my mother paid their bills and lived proper. I loved them for being so dull. They never read and never listened to Alexander Nicholas Scriabin's Poem of Fire or Shostakovitch's sad last few string quartets. (I could never figure why Dimitry never left Russia. He let the government dictate to him and he still created music that was original despite the censorship. It is hard to imagine leaving the country you love because of the danger of a military government.)

Bella Bartok languished in New York. He missed his home so much he died brokenhearted in a country that he never quite fit into. He loved Hungary.

It is obvious I have too much time on my hands. I have never typed so much and so fast.

Mozart could live no other place than Vienna. Beethoven loved Germany. The great German writer, Thomas Mann, never forgave Hitler for ruining his country. In "Doctor Faustus", Thomas Mann repeats his forlorn love for the country that he had to escape from to stay alive.

I recently reread forty or fifty books on world war II and became amazed that such a portentous event in human history happened so few years ago. Hitler and Stalin were responsible for over 100 million deaths on the earth. That a large group of people could allow such demons of degradation sway, benumbs me. The insanity of camps and extermination simply erases all history of human gentleness. I do not believe it can be made up even if Karma is fact. Each time I eat or enjoy the freedoms I have, I am wary of remembrance of the many who had it all taken away from them so quickly while the world seemed to allow it. I believe most of those people went insane before the effects of starvation and abuse killed them. I would not have wanted to be a psychologist in a death camp.

My family left the hills of Lebanon prior to world war I. My great grandfathers all came to America or died trying.

I was born in America and have never left. I have never felt connected to the old world, only the old ways.
I hope I have not overstepped by writing so much. I look forward to seeing if we have some email tangents, if you are willing to try.

Yours Truly

Ms. Cornelia

First of all I like your smile. Second I like that you are artistic or a photographer. Third I sense an intelligence or sensitivity about you through your profile and pictures.

I have found the process of match. com or eharmony to have a learning curve for me, trying to figure out how to introduce myself to someone.

I write poetry at this free web site. They do not bother the navigator with too much advertising and I find the process of writing poetry very fulfilling. I do not think that any of my attempts at matching have resulted in anyone reading my poems. I believe most people get turned off by my picture. I have lost over 38 pounds and continue to not add it back. I have about eighty pounds left and I will be at my proper weight by December. I do not exercise - yet. I have been losing the weight slowly by reducing my eating habits. It works fine for me at present. Years ago I did triathlons but I left off with the heavy intensity of exercise as my CPA business grew. Now, I am happy and complacent, but able to lose weight and maybe start a small exercise program as part of the next phases of losing weight. I am an intelligent and witty man and will tell you more if you wish to tell me more about yourself and show me some of your photographs.

Poem For January Thirteen

At Four On The Morning

I collect myself into a series of yawns
There is ambivalence in my heart
With no expectations of rewards
Since god and my ex-wife are asleep.
It is my favorite time to avoid being judged.
I left god on a battlefield in Vietnam
Where disbelief overcame my religion.
I left my wife in joy
Where finality never felt better.
The war over a South Asian country
Always felt wrong especially in the face
Of Frances defeat at Dien Bien Phu
My marriage always felt wrong because
She was never a friend, only a companion.
My children were right, as all children are,
As we all hold pride in their presence forever.
On this advent of a new year, I yawn and
Go back to sleep with this poem.

He/She

She:
turn on the lights
partake of me
our time is tonight
to give it to me
breathlessly
on bended knee
I lick salaciously
let your mind's eye
taste all of me

He:
darken my shaded eyes
to the upbringing skies
as night is my guide
to the banquet drain
of vespers of you

She:
Caress me
Undress me
Confess to me
I read your
throbbing thoughts
to be inside me
your feelings singe
with desire for me
I want you bare
utterly sincere
needing you here
beneath me; thighs spread
making me sigh for thee
to be a part of me

He:
Slicing incisively
those tight blossomed breasts
engaged by rigidity of pointedness
I wait for your commanding cries

She:
embrace me
take me
baptize me
release pent up
desire within me
peeling lace
from between
hungry thighs
pleading with
lascivious sighs
cries of pleasure
as tongue parts me

He:
Your dark deviltry
scintillating ebony
an ancient born black
token unearthed by lips
wrestling into tongued taste

She:
the feel of you
against skin
fingers web
as we begin
our horny sin
burns within
with parted lips
whispered inveigling
raising hips
with each thrust
colliding lips

meet firm phallus
with each graze
upon clit
fingertips invade
wet tightness
setting mind and
body ablaze
in so, many ways
with tremors
of lust and passion
leaves me breathless
in a delicious daze
amazed at the way
you make my body
sway with you
planting kisses
from ear to waist
in a hungry haste
not one kiss misplaced
still peeling lace
with finger tipped
grace; burying face
in your sweet space

He:
opened into pseudo spaces
of litanies of lustiness you
do not deny the lift of your hips
astride my pyre of moaning

it is me dissolved
it is me entangled
within you in trust

A New Year's Poem

Calm pervades
Eyes screen gray semblances
Fingers loosen thinned threads of emptiness
It was only yesterday that I loved you
I am resigned to your disappearance
In little cubes of thoughts, you sifted between the rocks gathered in stillness
Here is where your breath left a vapor on my neck
Here a sense of your body wilted to garlands of aching
Why did the excitement of you become so lonely
I will change the dates of forgetting
Before angels entangle themselves in sleep
I will become a spirit of forgiveness, taking away what pain is left over
and wish you a new year built upon
so many yesterdays
of love

A Short Snippet Of My Father, Mike Ferris

It was winter. Dad was in the front seat. Ma needed something from the grocery store. I let her off at the front door and parked out of traffic.

My father was a person of few words. I used to attribute it to his lack of schooling. He worked all his life keeping his family of nine fed. I assumed he was asleep leaning against the car window. People were passing huddled over from the weather.

"Look at that one. A real love machine. "

"Dad! I thought you were asleep. "

"I thought you were asleep.

Did you see the ass on that one ?"

When my dad could no longer take care of himself, I used to give him his bath. I commented to him, "Dad where the hell did you get such a big penis? He laughed and told me to be grateful that he used it to give me life.

Maybe Telemachus washed his old weak father Odysseus and asked him the same thing. Or, If Ernest Hemingway had a son to help him over old age, he would have avoided suicide. Who knows? Here was my dad needing a wheel chair and stretching past age eight five and still consumed by sex. A man who was still "well endowed". I guess sex stays with us till the end. Maybe men who are misogynist get their penis measured at the last judgment.

Self-Perception

I am never what I believe I want to be
Because I fall short in every area
I sleep on a precipice of acknowledgement
I wake with a blind eye toward my desires
Every time the mirror opens I turn away
And forget everything I know once more

A poem of nocturne by Michael Thomas
Between an alabaster moon and night
There is sweet nectar of music
Turning out the curfew of sounds
Into quiet peace by Chopin who
Left us to pray in his private world

She Who Died Little Known

Damned her and her primitive family
Who failed themselves and her in every way
Deserting her, abusing her, leaving her
To figure things out in her angelic way
That some god ignored and took her son
Took her life and health into a sinkhole
Where she forgot love and fought the pain
Until she forgot who she was under oxygen

A Poem of Redemption

Color me a traitor to crucifixion's promise
I believe only in a religion of fixing-things
To make amends by repetition of sorrows
A going over and over the same reading
Until the words take me into their meaning
And here you read me between grammar
As punctuated, spell-checked and deleted

Section Six –

Short Story

The Blood Widows

And Brahma: Brahmavihara

Brahma gave back scratchers to the blood widows as gifts. They tolerated them, never denying that the razor edges could save them in close combat. He was amused with their banter as they drove with him in the back seat weaving through busy streets of traffic. He reminded himself, constantly, that the widows could turn quickly into death machines on the spur of a moment. They had little compunction to taking life. Grace never drove. She preferred watching with her short stubby fingers clutching her purse and warning Anita of streets she could have taken to avoid the jams. Anita would always answer with a waving of her hand, "Yea".

Brahma thought that either of them could have been Madea who slayed her children to avenge her husband, Jason's indiscretions. The widows giggled. They spurned antiquity or any of the knowledge that Brahma, their brother, embraced. "Maybe you should marry a Buddha", they would say to him and laugh uproariously. They were sedate plain women who cut and styled their own hair. Anita dressed for comfort, Grace dressed for style. They both were well-off but accepted the Brahma paying for dinner and giving them tokens of his generosity.

Detective Sargent Mundane had sent Brahma a location of a murder on East Grand Boulevard in Detroit. Brahma was reflecting on the facts as his sisters playfully argued in the front seats. Mundane had said, "The victim was found at the bottom of stairs leading to the basement. She was naked, but for a bathrobe half off with her right leg twisted over her torso. Death seemed to come from a head injury as she fell. "

"What's the case?" Anita shouted back to him.

"Woman murdered. "

"By whom?"

"Don't know. She was the manager of the home for elderly, and was not too well liked. "

"So the old folks hated her and killed her?" Both blood widows laughed.

"Keep your eyes on the road and be nice when we get there. "

Anita: "Ugh hugh"

While they drove, Brahma begun to silently repeat:

"O what can ail thee, knight-at-arms,
  Alone and palely loitering?
The sedge is withered from the lake,
  And no birds sing. "

Brahma loved Keats and the meaning of the poem seemed to fit his mood.

Anita: "Just what are you mumbling back there, Brahma?"

Brahma: "Nothing, Just a Keats poem. "

Blood Widows (together in unison): "Keats! Go to sleep. Go to sleep. "

The car arrived at the nursing home, abuzz with police cars and an ambulance waiting for their dead passenger.

Mundane: "Brahma. Thank you for coming. I see we have the honor of your sisters. "

Blood Widows: (together) "Detective Mundane"

Brahma: "Can we see the body before they take it away?"

Brahma was rather surprised by the face of the corpse - a beautiful woman who had kept appearances with coiffured hair, well dressed and a slight drip of sweat leaving a trail from her eye to the chin.

Brahma: "I thought she would be older. "

Mundane: "Yes"

Blood Widow Grace: "Detective Mundane, may we get a sample of her blood, please?"
Mundane: "Okay, but the coroner will supply you with what you need during the examination of the body. "
Brahma: "Mundane, why does there seem to be a smell coming from her? Grace or Anita, can you identify the smell?"
They both shook their head negative. Brahma made notes while surveying the area around the body and he looked closely at the eyes of the gathered patients for any recognition of a clue to who her killer was. He came up blank; Shut his notebook; Walked back to the car with his eyes downward in contemplation.
It was said that Keats wrote "La Belle Dame sans Merci" to depict a beautiful woman with a dangerous side to her beauty. The Circe-like nature of her befalls the knight to his death. The Dame, like the corpse he had just seen, were both one to his imagination. He could not rid himself of the allurement of the corpse, even in her death-mask look. He could not but wonder who would want this woman dead.
Brahma adjusted the light shining onto the wall. Photographs and Post-It notes were linked with magic marker lines connecting possible suspects in a haphazard group.
Blood Widow Anita: "A home full of old people and a beautiful woman dead. Does not make sense to me. Look at the ages of all these people. Most of them should be dead instead of hanging around half-alive. "
Blood Widow Grace: "Half alive as you and I?"
Blood Widow Anita: "Speak for yourself. I still have some of my original teeth. "
Blood Widow Grace: "Your mouth is so full of root-canals, your x-rays could be mistaken for the city of Venice. "
Brahma: "Did you two notice that there are three cooks and a maintenance man working in the home? Let's take a look at their R&I. "

Blood Widow Grace: "Records & Identification for all of the people?"
Brahma: "No! Just the cooks and janitor guy. "

Author's Biography:

Writer, philosopher, philanthropist Michael Thomas is a long-time CPA from Canton, Michigan and a fine poet. We "discovered" him languishing in an online poetry site, writing who knows what to who knows whom. To our great satisfaction, he has taken to publishing his words, and the world is all the richer for it. Here he is doing an impersonation of a Detroit Mafia Hitman.

Also by Michael Thomas

ISBN: 978-1500192037

ISBN: 978-1492297567

ISBN: 978-1500267889

ISBN: 978-1492776932

ISBN: 978-1495419010

ISBN-13: 978-1501063275

ISBN: 978-1507634387

ISBN: 978-1514174104

ISBN-13:978-1523266333

These and other books by independent authors can be found at:

www. shoestringbookpublishing. com

Shoestring Book Publishing offers simple and affordable quality book publishing.

The smart choice for the wise independent authors voice!

Send your inquiry today to:
Shoestringpublishing4u@gmail. com
Contact Allan 207-922-8837
or Alison 732-331-7863

Please Review!

All independent authors depend upon reviews left on Amazon. com by readers to help promote their books. Without these reviews, they will hardly get any notice. Please take the time to leave a short review. Simply go to Amazon. com, find the book and go to the book's page. Under thc author's name will be a list of reviews and stars. Click here and there will be a big button saying "Create your own review". Please click here and review.

It only takes a minute!

www.ingramcontent.com/pod-product-compliance
Lightning Source LLC
Chambersburg PA
CBHW070641310726
48982CB00001B/372
9781943974078